BLACK OBSIDIAN

MARK RIDLER

BLACK OBSIDIAN

LitPrime Solutions
21250 Hawthorne Blvd
Suite 500, Torrance, CA 90503
www.litprime.com
Phone: 1 (209) 788-3500

Published by LitPrime Solutions   05/14/2021

ISBN: 978-1-954886-53-7(sc)
ISBN: 978-1-954886-54-4(e)

Library of Congress Control Number: 2021909736

CONTENTS

OXFORD-CENTRIC

L eather Jacket Man (or LJM for short) was bipolar. He suffered great swings from mania to depression and back again.

In the present case, he was in Littlemore Mental Health Centre with a dose of mania. He'd been hearing voices and seeing hallucinations, which are the hallmarks of psychosis. On the way to being picked up by the police, he talked to Prince Charles via a convenient tree and talked to the birds who were expressing themselves in a tweety variant of English. Even in the police car, he was counting aliens in passing cars. And he was stark naked.

Once in hospital, they gave him some clothes, and they adjusted his antipsychotic medication, putting him on 150-milligram paliperidone instead of 100 milligrams.

He was still on a range of other medication: 1,000 milligrams of lithium mood stabiliser and 100 milligrams of sertraline antidepressant.

Later on that day, he was having a medical and was being asked to stand on the bathroom scales, which he did.

'Blimey, I'm half a stone lighter,' he said.

'Your body mass index [BMI] is well within the healthy range, so I wouldn't worry,' said the doctor.

Theofanes Raptor was pondering life and the universe. As a trained physicist with a background in software engineering, he had more than enough credentials to contemplate the big questions.

A favourite website of his was Wikipedia, with its list of unsolved problems in physics. This included, amongst other things, dark matter and dark energy.

A more speculative area of physics was known as negative mass. The theoretical groundwork for this had been done in the 1950s by Hermann Bondi.

Whereas the discovery of antimatter in the 1930s was standard science.

Theo reasoned that if known matter and antimatter both had positive mass, then there could well be negative mass variants out there. Negative mass with negative energy would contribute to four roots of the Dirac equation, as per Don Hotson in the *Infinite Energy* magazine.

This was consistent with a variant of physics from Dr Jamie S. Farnes of Oxford University. In Jamie's universe, dark matter and dark energy have a common origin as a dark fluid with negative mass.

Little did Theo know that things on the ground were well- advanced. As well as studying negative mass in a laboratory, a start-up company on the Begbroke Science Park called New Age Technologies was planning on making the stuff—for real.

There was some speculation as to what the properties of such an exotic substance might be, ranging from antigravity to total annihilation. This meant that self-propelling spaceships or the negative mass (NM) bomb (more powerful than a nuclear bomb) would be real possibilities. Either way, the show would be worth the entry price.

Henning Horlicks had decided to go back to his home country of Canada. He could make improvements to his quantum entanglement (QE) machine and study its effects perfectly well from there.

This left an existing QE machine in Exeter in the UK, under the watchful eye of MI5.

Henning had a family, a wife and two children, so he preferred to stay at home if he could. Project Blue Crystal had been a real strain, taking him away from his family for an extended period of time, but thankfully, that was over now.

Likewise, Kingsley Khan was now operating his electromagnetic (EM) machine back in Australia. He had the benefit of EM south being in his homeland, albeit with Alice Springs being a considerable distance from his native Sydney.

Kingsley operated a mobile variant of his EM machine called SuperCamper. This had the benefit of doubling up as a camper van if he wanted to drive it through the outback. This was left over from the Blue Crystal operation.

Kingsley was single, so there were no restrictions on travelling for him. He still preferred to be close to his parents though.

Julia Barnes had hung up her CIA hat and put on an MI5 one instead. She was still actively employed whilst the British continued to track down the effects of the Khan EM and the Horlicks QE machines.

Julia was still single, having not met the perfect man yet. She aspired to settle down and raise a family, but it just hadn't happened for her yet.

'Theo, it's Julia. How are you?'

'Not too bad. Thanks. It's been a while,' he replied.

'Yes, it has. I should phone more often. Did you have any thoughts on the Oxford set-up?' she asked.

'There's little doubt that this will be the source of new physics if and when it arrives. They're actually proposing to make the stuff here on Earth, not just study it out in the cosmos,' he postulated.

'Jeepers. I think it will be well worth a visit then,' she asserted.

'Will you be coming along too? Two heads are always better than one.'

'Yes, we can make a day of it.'

Julia drove from London to Oxford with Theo in the passenger seat. She still had her little Smart car, which was perfect for this sort of occasion.

First stop was Bicester Village, where she bought a Gucci handbag.

'I didn't think we came to Oxford to go shopping,' complained Theo.

'I just couldn't resist,' said Julia truthfully.

Next, she stopped at Peartree services, which is in the north off the A34. She got out and held a finger to the wind.

'There's a rumour that the wind constantly blows to the east if you're north of Oxford and to the west if you're to the south,' she said.

'No way!' he responded.

'Yes way!' she confirmed. 'Though I'm not normally one for conspiracy theories.'

'Well, we're in plenty of time for our appointment. How about we have a coffee first then drive south around the ring road?' he proposed.

'Done,' she agreed.

Inside Starbucks, Theo ordered a small black Americano, and Julia ordered a tall skinny latte. They sat down in the comfy- ish chairs and relaxed.

'So what do we expect from Jamie S. Farnes? Or New Age Technologies?' asked Theo.

'I really have no idea. We're here to find out,' replied Julia. 'Why don't you take this opportunity to tell me a little bit about yourself, seeing as I know very little?' she added.

'Uh, OK. I was born and raised in Greece. Went to university in Greece. Democritus. Worked for a while in Athens before moving to the USA. Then transferred to the UK as part of the Blue Crystal project,' responded Theo.

'And what about you? What do you like doing?' she elaborated.

'Eat pies. Sleep a lot. Drink Tango,' he joked. 'Actually, I prefer drinking beer.'

Back outside, they agreed they would travel east around the ring road in the alleged direction of the wind.

They drove past the BMW Mini plant and took the Cowley exit signposted to the retail park.

'There's a Costa inside Tesco's,' suggested Theo.

'You can't seriously want another coffee already!' she exclaimed.

'No, but they do Belgian chocolate tiffins.' He grinned.

Either way, when she got out of the car, Julia judged that the wind was indeed blowing to the west.

'Well, the conspiracy theory is right! Shall we attribute it to strange new physics?' she joked.

'Why not ask Jamie Farnes?' suggested Theo, taking it seriously.

'OK, I will,' said Julia soberly.

When it was time to make a move, they elected to take Cowley Road directly into town. Julia pulled over into the Shell garage to top up with fuel.

'Look, we can get Costa Express,' teased Theo. 'I'll knock your block off,' she threatened.

The rest of the journey to Parks Road was uneventful. Julia parked on Keble Road next to the computer science building and then walked across to the physics building with Theo.

When they got to reception, they were given temporary passes and guided to Lecture Theatre A.

Inside, they took seats at the front and waited for their host to arrive. They didn't wait for more than a few minutes.

'Hi, I'm Jamie Farnes, and you must be Julia.' She waved hi.

'And you must be Theo.' 'Pleased to meet you,' he said.

'Well, I'll kick off with my standard lecture, and we'll take it from there.'

His lecture covered the known problems of dark matter and dark energy before moving on to the more speculative properties of negative mass by Hermann

Bondi. He then finished by covering the cosmological data and presenting his theory of a dark fluid as a solution to both problems.

'What's your take on the rumours about wind direction on the Oxford ring road?' asked Julia.

'Purely coincidental,' came the reply.

'Could it be related to the work you're doing?' asked Theo.

'If it was, it would be centred on the Begbroke Science Park, where they're attempting to make negative mass.'

'That's our next destination,' said Julia.

Julia passed the sign for Yarnton: 5,000 Years of History.

'Oxford itself is only Saxon in origin, so where do they get 5,000 years from?' she complained.

She turned on to Begbroke Hill, which leads up to the Begbroke Science Park. She parked in the car park in front of the big blue building.

'Neat and tidy,' commented Theo.

'Do you mean my parking?' queried Julia.

'No, I meant the organisation of this place,' confirmed Theo. 'We'll see how they stack up,' she continued.

After introductions and formalities, Julia and Theo were given a briefing on what to expect by the CEO of New Age Technologies, Ross Grant.

Then they were shown the kit. This consisted of a tabletop particle accelerator and a similar-sized detector.

'We're further ahead with detecting negative mass than we are with making it. At the moment, our best results say that negative mass has been definitely detected within 100 miles of Oxford,' said Ross.

Theo and Julia looked at each other.

'We'd really like to have one of your detectors,' said Theo out loud.

'We'll be lucky,' muttered Julia.

LJM was filling his time in hospital by writing. Firstly, as emails from his phone and then on WordPress when he had a chance to access the computer under the supervision of Stacey, the young nurse.

One post in particular was called 'A Winston Churchill Day', where LJM recounted the story of how he'd visited WC's grave at 6 a.m. on a Sunday morning and had a thoroughly manic day from there on. It ended with him ditching his car and walking two of the three miles into town, taking a taxi for the last mile.

When he reached a convenient point, he had it published as his memoir: *Write and Burn: Adventures in Bipolar Mania*.

When Julia got back to base at Thames House, she made the decision to put in a request for a copy of the detector she and Theo had seen at the Begbroke Science Park.

She sat down with her boss, Giles Rutherford.

'Yesterday, we were privileged to witness some new physics. The concept of negative mass has moved beyond the theoretical to the physical. Although we still can't produce the stuff, we have a working detector now. With your help, I think we should put some pressure on the start-up company to produce a second detector as a matter of priority for use by MI5,' she explained.

'And what do you propose doing with it?' he asked naturally.

'We're told that negative mass has been detected within 100 miles of Oxford. We could put some more measurements on the map and hopefully discover some more,' she replied.

'And what specification of detector do you want?' he asked.

'Literally a copy of what they've got right now. We want whatever is easiest and quickest for them to produce,' she expanded.

'OK, I'll get right on to it.'

When Giles made the request on behalf of Julia, it landed on the prime minister's desk.

'New physics?' exclaimed Theresa May.

'So it seems,' said her advisor. 'This hasn't been peer- reviewed yet, so we can't be too sure of the results, never mind the conclusion.'

'Negative mass detected within 100 miles of Oxford. So that could be in London,' she added.

'We'll get MI5 to make a specific measurement for London as soon as they have their own detector,' he advised.

'The Americans will want one too,' she pointed out. 'They don't have to hear about it just yet,' he surmised.

With that, Donald Trump got on the phone with Theresa May.

'Theresa, what's this we hear about negative mass being detected within 100 miles of Oxford? What's negative mass? A bit like something you can eat that makes you lighter?' he demanded.

'We don't know for sure. This is all before it's been peer- reviewed. But yes, for what it's worth, we have an initial result centred on Oxford.'

'Why Oxford?' he asked.

'Because that's where the Begbroke Science Park is,' she responded.

'We want one of those detectors you're using,' he said simply. 'What do we have to do to get our hands on one of those?'

'We'll arrange for you to have one. It will be delivered to the American Embassy,' she explained.

'Bingo,' he replied.

'This project will be known as Black Obsidian,' stated Theresa. 'Why?' he asked.

'Because obsidian is coloured black, and you use it to gaze into the future,' she emphasised.

'Oh, OK,' said Donald.

'Well, we had to get one back on you after Blue Crystal,' she explained. 'I'm calling the shots this time.'

'Blue Crystal was my erstwhile predecessor's baby,' he stated. 'And mine,' she responded.

The next thing to happen was that Thames House took delivery of a brand-new NM detector. It was exactly the same, except it was sensitive up to a distance of 50 miles.

'Shall we give it a go?' asked Giles.

'How do we operate it?' asked Julia sensibly. 'There's a cheat sheet here,' said Giles.

'I think I'd rather get the Mongols in on this. Sorry to put a spoiler on things,' said Julia.

At the same time, the American Embassy took delivery of their detector. With nobody to operate it, it sat languishing in the basement until the CIA arrived to ship it off to mainland USA.

Julia got in contact with Henning and Kingsley and explained to them the urgency of the situation given that new physics was involved. They both agreed to travel to the UK right away.

In the event, Henning showed up first whilst Kingsley was delayed for another twenty-four hours. Julia elected to go ahead with just Henning and Theo on board.

Henning took the cheat sheet and read it carefully.

'According to this, we need to check the levels here, here, and here,' he said. 'Then we switch to engage here.' A hissing noise emanated from the machine. 'Then we switch it on and wait for twenty-four hours.'

'That long?' queried Julia.

'Yep. Seems so,' answered Henning.

'How do we get the results out?' asked Theo.

'USB cable to a phone or laptop,' answered Henning again.

When Kingsley turned up later that evening, Julia decided to treat them all to some good food. They went to the Clarendon Royal Hotel restaurant nearby Thames House. They went inside, and after dispensing their hats and coats, they sat down at the table.

'So, Kingsley, how has it been for you in Australia?' Julia asked.

'More of the same, really. I've been conducting experiments and following the trails,' he responded.

'Did you have anything more to do with LJM? It was weird him showing up in the bar in Alice Springs at the exact same time we did,' she asked further.

'No, I let him be. I figured he'd had enough hassle in his life by that point. I think they stayed in Australia for a couple of weeks before going back to the UK,' he continued.

'And did you get any results from your experiments?' she pushed.

'Yes, I deduced that Patsy, the barmaid, has the same status in EM south that LJM does in EM north. She represents the end of a biological signal,' he answered.

'Wicked,' said Henning, joining the conversation.

'Yes, it sounds really significant,' said Theo, not wishing to be left out.

When the results were ready on Henning's experiment in Thames House, it showed no negative mass within 50 miles of London.

'Well, that's interesting,' said Theo. 'It would almost be worth redoing the Oxford result to confirm.'

'I think we should invest our efforts in new measurements. How about north, south, east, and west of Oxford?' declared Julia.

Kingsley consulted the map on his phone. 'Like Nottingham, Southampton, Southend, and Hereford. We would expect Southend to come back null given the London result, but it would still be interesting to do it.'

'Agreed,' said Julia. 'Now all we need to do is put the detector in the back of a van.'

'It needs a 240-volt power supply and a level, vibration-free surface,' said Henning.

'And', said Julia, 'we won't be operating it whilst moving along.'

'I'd check with Giles first before risking the detector,' said Theo.

Giles was duly notified and gave the OK. NM van was a go-go.

The small amount of work to install a generator was done, and the detector was mounted in the back.

First up, it was Henning's turn to drive to Nottingham.

He consulted the satnav but didn't really need to because it was straight up the M1.

The drive was straightforward, and he checked in to the Travelodge when he got there. It was then that he got a real surprise because he realised that he had to keep the engine running to keep the generator turning. This would hardly be vibration-free and would keep everyone in the hotel awake at night.

'Muppets,' he muttered under his breath.

Henning stayed the night without making a measurement and drove back in the morning.

'This isn't good enough,' he said to Giles.

Giles responded by having the detector converted from 240 volts AC to 12 volts DC so it could run off car batteries. His electrician calculated that five batteries were sufficient for twenty-four hours, so a pack of six allowed room for error.

Henning asked whether the batteries were definitely charged before setting off to Nottingham once again.

This time, the system operated flawlessly. With batteries running in silence, Henning was happy to leave it operating during the night and throughout the next day in the Travelodge car park.

When the time came, he downloaded the result, and it told him that negative mass was detected within 50 miles of Nottingham.

Henning was at once delighted with the result and disappointed that it didn't go further.

When Julia was on the phone with Henning, she informed him of the new project name. 'Obsidian mirrors are used for seeing into the future. It's also known as scrying and is something witches do,' she reported.

'Well, that will be useful,' he replied sarcastically.

When Henning got back to base, he swapped drivers with Kingsley.

Kingsley had a similar uncomplicated journey down the M3 to Southampton. He set off right away.

It was getting dark by the time he got there. He was following the signs to the docks when he was forced off the road by a black van with no licence plates.

He was dragged out of his white van at gunpoint, had a grey hood shoved over his head, and was detained in the back of the black van.

'Who are you?' he demanded. 'Why am I here?'

'Shut up with the questions,' came the curt reply. 'What's Black Obsidian?'

'It's the code name for our project.' 'Which does what?'

'You wouldn't understand,' asserted Kingsley.

'We know the machine in your van is a negative-mass detector. You're going to tell us all about it.'

LJM meanwhile had made the transition from manic to depressed, so there was little risk of the psychotic symptoms that had put him in the hospital in the first place. The staff were very pleased with how much progress he'd made in the space of a month.

Shortly, LJM got himself out of mental hospital and back to work. He was employed as a software engineer in the Computer Science Department in Oxford, just across from the physics building. He walked down Keble Road every day. This was a level of spookiness unknown to MI5 at the time.

Kingsley was left by the side of the road with an empty van.

'Well, the only person I've spoken to aside from the Mongols is Giles. But he's probably talked to several because I know for a fact that the project name came from the prime minister,' she said.

Julia got off the phone, and Theo approached her desk.

'There is another explanation,' he said. 'That all of this is a hoax designed to put us off the scent whereas something else is really going on.'

'Conspiracy theory noted,' she replied. 'In the absence of any other information, we'll continue to operate as if negative mass is real. I'm sure we didn't just get mugged on a hoax.'

'Stranger things have happened. It just makes it seem more real if someone else wants it too. This has echoes of the cold fusion scandal from the 1980s,' he surmised.

'In the absence of our own measurements, pretty much all I can do is report this up the chain and chase Oxford for more results,' she concluded.

Giles took it on board that they had a leak. And given that the Americans had been notified, it was possible that they were the source of the leak. Needless to say, they denied CIA involvement in the heist.

Julia contacted New Age Technologies and was given the latest result, which was that negative mass had been detected within 25 miles of Oxford.

'Can't we narrow that down any more?' she complained. 'Believe me, we're doing everything we can,' came the reply. Then Julia took an unexpected call to her landline.

'If you want your detector back, it will cost you a million pounds. In used £5 notes. Non-sequential numbers. To be left in your van in Heathrow car park terminal 4,' said a raspy voice.

'I get the detector first, then you get your money,' she asserted in return.

'Deal. Midnight tonight.' Then the caller hung up.

'Well, that was an unexpected turn of events,' she exclaimed. She phoned Giles.

'No deal,' he said. 'We can get a new one for less than that. It will be here in less than a week.'

'Fair enough.'

When the new detector arrived, it had the latest specification of twelve miles.

'This is starting to be more useful,' said Henning.

Kingsley volunteered to drive the van back to Southampton even though the other three were up for a driver change given the traumatic experience of last time.

Julia wasn't happy, and she said so to Giles. She was overruled.

So Kingsley got to drive again, this time making it to the Travelodge car park without incident.

When he took the measurement, it told him that negative mass was detected within 12 miles of Southampton.

This time, Kingsley was done over on the way back from Southampton in broad daylight.

'You won't believe it, Julia. They've done it again,' he fumed.

'Something is very wrong about the way we're operating. Giles will have to listen this time,' she explained.

Matters went over Giles's head and landed squarely on the prime minister's desk.

'So it seems we have a persistent terrorist threat. Apparently motivated by money but likely confident they can ambush us any time they want,' she said.

'I'd recommend a military escort in front and behind, assuming it's important we keep doing this. And send military protection for New Age Technologies. We've all been sleepwalking into this one,' said the Home Secretary.

'Well, it's all a question of whether you believe in new physics or not,' said Theresa. 'Some will believe it come what may, and others will say it's a conspiracy theory regardless.'

'We've got no choice until the peer-review process kicks in. I understand that New Age Technologies have just published a paper in *Infinite Energy* magazine,' he added.

'That's not a peer-reviewed journal,' she hissed.

'Perhaps they've done it deliberately to stall for time,' he mused. 'I'll see if I can apply some pressure.'

By this time, the general public had wind that something was afoot. They'd heard the rumours about negative mass in Oxford and could see the military checkpoint on the entrance to the Begbroke Science Park.

They started to accumulate with placards.

'No to negative mass!' 'Annihilation, here we come!' 'Not in Oxford!'

All this led the military to up security. All phone calls in or out were blocked, and access to the latest information was severely restricted.

Meanwhile, the Mongols got to complete their set of measurements in Hereford and Southend-on-Sea, albeit under the watchful eyes of a military escort. They were banned from telephoning the results to anyone, so the flow of information was strictly limited to the chain of command.

This meant that the only people who knew the Hereford result were Theo and Julia. Henning and Kingsley were kept out of the loop.

The result was that no negative mass was detected within six miles of Hereford. This seemed a far cry from narrowing in on the 100-mile result from Oxford because the detectors had improved so much since then.

The Southend result was similar—a no-show.

So what was it about Oxford, Nottingham, and Southampton? Theo and Julia were at a loss. At least with the improving detectors, they had a chance of zeroing in some more.

Giles visited Julia at her desk. 'Can we go into the boardroom?' he asked.

'Sure,' she replied.

'I have a new piece of information for you. The next detectors from New Age Technologies will have the ability to detect the amount of negative mass as well as the overall range,' he explained. 'We want you to redo the Nottingham and Southampton results and put in a new measurement in Oxford to back up what New Age Technologies are saying.'

By this time, the latest detector had a distance of three miles. Henning and Kingsley were called upon to drive to Nottingham and Southampton once again given they were familiar with the destinations.

Henning reported his result to Julia when he got back to Thames House. 'There is minus one and a half kilograms of negative mass within three miles of Nottingham Travelodge Central,' he announced.

'Wow, that's not much. It makes it much less likely to be a geographical feature,' she countered.

'Could we be looking at a person?' he asked.

'I don't know who it would be in Nottingham,' she mused.

'Is it possible that the Southampton and Oxford results are also people?' he wondered out loud.

When Kingsley brought in the Southampton Travelodge Central result, Julia found out it was also for minus one and a half kilograms.

Finally, Theo did the drive to Oxford and established that minus three kilograms of negative mass was there too.

'So we're looking at two people in Oxford,' he said.

'Assuming it's minus one and a half kilograms per person,' she responded.

'Who on earth could it be?' he asked. Theo and Julia looked at each other. 'LJM,' they both said at the same time.

They were both familiar with LJM from the Blue Crystal operation.

'I'll look him up in the system,' she said.

Sure enough, it turned out LJM was in Oxford.

'Well, that's prime suspect number 1. What were the chances of that?' she concluded.

'Giles, I have reason to believe these minus one and a half kilograms negative-mass detections are people rather than places. Our prime suspect is the man at the centre of the EM signal called Leather Jacket Man, or LJM for short, who also happens to be in Oxford,' Julia explained.

'Assuming you're right, what do you want me to do? Bring him in?' he asked.

'Send a military escort to pick him up and bring him to Thames House so we can do an experiment,' she said simply.

LJM was busy writing his next book titled *Black Obsidian*. He was sitting in the same Starbucks at Peartree services that Theo and Julia had stopped in, typing into his phone.

An armoured car pulled up in the coach park. Two soldiers got out whilst a third remained on guard.

The soldiers walked into the entrance lobby in between Waitrose and Starbucks. They were clearly looking for someone.

LJM got up to leave but was intercepted. 'You need to come with us, sir.'

'Am I under arrest?' LJM retorted.

'Not as such. It's classed as a national emergency,' came the cryptic response.

'Are we going to the Begbroke Science Park?' He'd seen the news.

'London.'

When LJM arrived at Thames House, everyone breathed a sigh of relief that he wasn't blown up by a landmine or worse; such was the perceived terrorist threat.

'We need you to hang around in this office for the next twelve hours. Food and drink will be provided. Do you think you can do that?' asked Julia.

LJM agreed.

He spent most of his time either on his phone or pacing around the office.

When the result was in, it was taken directly from Henning to Giles. Negative mass had been detected to the tune of minus one and a half kilograms.

Giles instructed the military to take LJM into custody. 'What did I do?' complained LJM loudly.

Julia organised a meeting in the boardroom. Giles was present, plus the three Mongols—Theo, Henning, and Kingsley.

'The big news of the day is that LJM just tested positive for negative mass. This means that at least one of the signals is a person rather than a place,' she said.

Henning and Kingsley looked at each other. 'It's possible they all are,' she continued. 'This is starting to sound familiar,' said Theo.

'Henning and Kingsley, your brief is to explain what impact these negative-mass results have on your EM and QE machines,' she concluded. 'You have three days.'

'This is top secret, gentlemen. Theories to be circulated in this room only,' said Giles.

'Can we confer? asked Henning.

'Yes, and please include Theo,' answered Giles.

LJM meanwhile was not enjoying life in a cell. At least they'd let him have his mobile phone so he could carry on with his story.

※

Julia and Giles were called to another top-secret meeting at New Age Technologies.

Ross delivered the news.

'We've got a lot to digest all in one go. Firstly, we made an attempt to publish in *Nature* and got rejected. Apparently, we don't qualify as the kind of new science they like to see in their journal. Unbelievable!' he exploded.

'Leave that one with us,' commanded Giles.

'Next up is the latest result, which is we're down to zero kilograms within one mile of the Begbroke Science Park. This means the three kilograms detected last time is most likely within Oxford itself,' said Ross.

Julia smiled to think that MI5 were a long way ahead on that one.

'Then we've got the news that our line of detectors will split into long distance and short distance. The current specs are 500 miles and one mile,' continued Ross.

'Can we have a long-distance one?' asked Julia. 'I'll sort that out,' said Giles.

'Finally, we've got the groundbreaking news that negative mass has been synthesised for the first time. Not enough yet to ascertain its properties but sufficient to be seen by the detector,' concluded Ross.

'That's definitely worth publishing in *Nature*. I'll lean on them to stop being silly,' finished Giles.

⎯⎯ ∿∘⊙⥈⊙⥈⊙∘∿ ⎯⎯

On the way back to London, Julia was quizzing Giles.

'Surely we should be sharing information with these people? They're at the cutting edge,' she quizzed.

'You would think so, but it would make them even more of a security risk. This way, we get to divide and conquer, and MI5 keeps its edge,' he reasoned.

⎯⎯ ∿∘⊙⥈⊙⥈⊙∘∿ ⎯⎯

Giles decided to get his counterpart in the CIA, Dawn Deacon, to assist.

'Dawn, it's Giles. I'll get right to the point. Our people at New Age Technologies are trying very hard to get their work published in *Nature* and are being unkindly rejected.'

'I know. It was us who pulled the plug. Are you sure you want to go public with this? It seems kind of sensitive,' she pointed out.

'The whole point is we're trying to get others to replicate our work. A straightforward article in a respected journal is the way to go,' he countered.

'What about the crowd-control angle?' she insisted.

'We've already got the military camped out at the Begbroke Science Park,' he reasoned.

'Well, if you're sure you want to go ahead, then we'll let it through,' she conceded.

'Thank you. I appreciate it,' he said.

Henning and Kingsley were ready to make their presentations in the boardroom.

Henning went first.

'On the face of it, negative mass appears to be independent of the QE machine. It works by generating quantum-entangled pairs with the effects seen by subjects as a flash of light or heard as a random noise. It may well be that negative mass is part of the way it works already. One thing I would like to do, which is something I've been asking for for a long time, is to ask LJM to cooperate as part of a QE experiment. Now that he's understood to be carrying negative mass, this should shed new light on any capability he has,' surmised Henning.

Kingsley went second.

'It isn't known how the EM machine works. One of the theories was that it separated into streams of positive and negative inertial mass. This seems more likely now that negative mass is real. In terms of where we go next, I'd like to take the EM machine back to Exeter with the NM detector. Then we can see whether we can measure the geographical feature as well as the people. Yes, it would be helpful to have LJM on board,' he postulated.

EXETER OPERATIONS

Henning went ahead with the experiment with the QE machine and LJM. First task was to get it out of mothballs, where it had been stored on the old basketball court at Wonford House in Exeter.

Dealing with the hardware was one thing. Dealing with the software was something else entirely because it had been handed over from the CIA to MI5. Fortunately, the software was managed by Theo in the USA and Exeter, so it was a small step to involve him now they were at MI5.

'Let me speak to the MI5 IT department, and we'll get up to speed to support you ASAP,' said Theo.

Kingsley faced a similar situation, except his machine was fully under military control. Trying to talk them into doing another EM experiment in Exeter was an exercise in futility.

'Are you completely mad? You'll set off another earthquake in Exeter and sink the newly rebuilt St Thomas church another five feet into the ground,' roared General Harry Piers.

'I'm proposing to use very low power, so the risks should be minimal,' countered Kingsley.

'And which venue do you propose using?' asked the General.

'St Thomas church ideally. I really need to be at the epicentre,' said Kingsley honestly.

The General choked on his tea. 'Mad. Barking mad.'

Kingsley put down his phone, a tad disappointed. He explained the situation to Julia, who spoke to Giles; and before the day was out, a memo was on the prime minister's desk.

Giles meanwhile had taken delivery of a long-range NM detector from New Age Technologies. 'It's good for 1,000 miles,' he said to himself, reading from the cheat sheet. He delegated to Julia to decide what to do with it.

The next thing to happen was the New Age Technologies article appearing in *Nature*. This had the immediate effect of tripling crowd numbers outside the Begbroke Science Park.

The reaction from the physics community was one of shock and disbelief with some excitement. Several establishments took it upon themselves to replicate their results.

The first establishment to declare a result was an American one called Black Obsidian. It was suspicious how quick off the mark they were. They declared that negative mass had been detected within 100 miles of New York. MI5 noted the coincidence with the project name and assumed that the CIA were pulling the strings.

Hot off the press was a new organisation called the Campaign for Negative Mass Disarmament (CNMD). They were demanding a total ban on research and development of negative mass for fear of it spiralling out of control.

Theresa May got on the phone to Donald Trump.

'Congratulations on finding some negative mass. And thank you for allowing the article to go out in *Nature*,' she said simply.

'It means we've now got the CNMD to deal with. And lord knows what the rest of the planet will find,' he cursed.

'But we remain several steps ahead. And we've got LJM in custody,' she pointed out.

'And who knows how many more like him there are,' he finished. Silence.

'There was one more thing. Our people are asking to do an EM experiment on the site of the St Thomas church meltdown in Exeter. It risks triggering off another earthquake. Do you have any views?' she queried.

'It's your own backyard. You do whatever you want,' he avoided.

'I just wondered whether there was any global concern considering the ramifications it all had last time,' she wondered.

'I don't work for Greenpeace. I'll let you know when I do,' he retorted.

⸻⁓⸺⸻

Kingsley was given the go-ahead by Julia, who in turn took her cue from Giles. Giles spoke to the military to sort out the disagreement.

He had to wait on the Royal Artillery to move his machine into place in St Thomas church. Before that could happen, a solid silver ground conductor was cast in place of some tiles that had been removed from the floor. Silver was the best conductor of electricity, so it enabled them to get the most out of the experimental results.

No sooner had they finished casting than Greenpeace turned up at the door.

'We've got intelligence to say that you're planning another earthquake-triggering type of experiment that caused the damage to this church the last time around. We're taking over this church on behalf of the people.'

The invaders were heavily armed, so the military let things go rather than get into combat. When Greenpeace saw the cast conductor, they realised that their intelligence was correct, which made them all the more determined to hold the church.

⁓⁓

It made the local and national news. 'Greenpeace holds up St Thomas church in armed conflict.'

'We're holding the St Thomas church to prevent an experiment that could bring earthquakes back to Exeter. We believe the Royal Artillery are working in collaboration with MI5 to cause untold destruction in this area. This must be stopped. If we could have taken the church by peaceful means, we would have done so. But the military are armed, so we must be too. We're not a terrorist organisation. We are part of Greenpeace.'

Greenpeace themselves denied the news, saying they were into peaceful protest only. It was a splinter group who were into armed protest.

The next day, the military returned in force.

'We don't want to harm you, but we want to get rid of the weapons. Leave them on the steps of the church and let this be a peaceful protest. If you force us to shoot our way in, we will. You have no hostages,' said the loudhailer.

Will Turing thought about it.

'OK, laying down arms now,' he said.

It was decided that Kingsley would be the best negotiator given that it was him who really wanted to go ahead with this experiment in the first place. So he had to go to Exeter and confront Will face-to-face.

'Will, my name is Kingsley. I'm in charge of this experiment,' said Kingsley.

'An experiment to do what?' replied Will.

'To measure positive versus negative mass in the vicinity,' explained Kingsley.

'So you're doing the same thing as New Age Technologies,' said Will.

'Similar. We're trying to correlate what happened here with the NM detector,' said Kingsley.

'But the NM detector works without a ground conductor. If you're casting in silver, then it can only mean you're planning on using the EM machine, which causes earthquakes,' said Will.

'Correct. But also wrong. The EM machine has only ever caused an earthquake once, and that was by using it on full power in Dartmoor. We're proposing to do a low-power experiment here in St Thomas, which should be perfectly benign,' said Kingsley.

'But you can't guarantee that,' said Will.

'I can't guarantee that there won't be a naturally occurring earthquake here in five minutes' time,' said

Kingsley. 'It's all about risk. The risk is minimal. I wouldn't be proposing it otherwise.'

'OK, but we get visibility of the method and the results.' 'Deal.'

Kingsley was keen to get on with things, so he contacted Lieutenant Tania Orion, who was still in charge of running EM machine operations.

'The machine will be delivered and assembled in the morning. We should be good to go by lunchtime,' she said.

This gave Kingsley the evening off, so he decided to visit 7 Wok, where he'd been before with Julia and Henning. By this time, it had turned into 10 Wok, where they were charging a tenner for a meal with drink included.

Afterwards, he walked around Cathedral Green and visited the Christmas market.

In the morning, Tania was on schedule.

'How will the software be handled?' he asked.

'Lieutenant John Wilkes did a handover from Theofanes Raptor. I can get him on the line if you want,' she replied.

'No, that's fine,' he responded.

When the time came, Tania took the controls.

'Remember, you're doing a fifteen-minute pulse at 1 per cent power,' he advised.

'Already taken account of. We did the download last night,' she ruled. 'This feels like we're tickling the chin of a dragon here.'

'The magma reservoir is under Dartmoor, so we're some way away here,' he pointed out.

'OK, I'm ready,' she declared.

'I shouldn't need to walk away on such low power,' he said confidently.

'Go,' she yelled.

Kingsley experienced a mild humming sound known as the Hum. The rest of Exeter would experience it too to a greater or lesser degree.

Tania was the only one completely insulated from the effects because she was sitting inside a Faraday cage as part of the machine set-up.

No earthquake had shown up by the end of the fifteen minutes.

Will was wide-eyed.

'Phew,' said Tania.

'Over to you for the results,' said Kingsley. 'It will take a day or so,' she advised.

'A day or so. Am I being cut out of the loop?' complained Will.

'No, I'll send you an encrypted email with the results,' assured Kingsley. 'Can I have your email address?'

Will supplied it.

'Let's break for lunch,' said Kingsley. 'How about Goa Spice? MI5 is paying the bill.'

Then Julia turned up, having driven the van from London to Exeter.

Kingsley introduced Tania and Will.

'Pleased to meet you, Tania. Pleased to meet you, Will. I'm Julia Barnes, MI5,' introduced Julia. 'I thought you could do with the long- and short-range NM detectors,' she exclaimed to Kingsley.

'No LJM?' asked Kingsley.

'Shush!' she answered. 'He's off-limits for this operation.'

'In that case, we don't need Tania and her team any further. We'll just do a measurement with the NM detector, and that will be that.'

They finished lunch and said their goodbyes. Will hung around.

'How long does this thing take?' asked Kingsley.

'A much more modest six hours,' replied Julia. 'We'll be done by this evening.' 'I've missed you,' she mused.

'I've missed you too,' he mused in return.

The inevitable happened, and Kingsley ended up back at Julia's hotel, but not before they had their measurements:

- −100 tons of negative mass within 1,000 miles of Exeter

- −1.5 kilograms of negative mass within three miles of Exeter

'This is sounding more like a geographical feature on the long-range result. The short-range result appears to identify another person.'

They waited another day and took the EM result from Lieutenant John Wilkes.

'It shows almost no horizontal signal apart from a weak detection in the direction of Crediton but a strong vertical signal going straight down into the earth,' said Kingsley.

He wondered whether his machine was showing the same results as the NM detector but in a more detailed format.

'We'll need another experiment in Crediton if we want to track down who that is,' he said.

Henning meanwhile had the authorisation to go ahead with LJM. They took the trip to Exeter together on the train and then got a taxi to Wonford House.

Henning set up the QE machine and yelled 'Go' when he pressed the switch.

Both he and LJM were hit with a wall of random noise and flashes of light.

Henning ran it for thirty seconds and then switched it off. 'Did you get anything?' he asked LJM.

'I heard one voice,' he replied cryptically. 'Whose?'

'Yours.'

ALIENS ARE AMONGST US

Giles and Julia were called to another top-secret meeting at New Age Technologies.

Ross Grant was the bearer of news.

'We've improved our long-range detector to the point where it can measure all the way to the centre of the earth. So it's good for 6,000 miles. The result came back that there is a whopping minus million million million tons of the stuff, which is a substantial portion of the earth's core. So the planet as a whole has both positive and negative masses.

'And we've got the good news that our synthesis of negative mass has allowed its properties to be measured. It forms a superposition of antigravity and annihilation. So both self- propelling spaceships and negative-mass bombs are on the cards, if we can make enough of it,' said Ross. 'I wouldn't be quite as direct as that in *Nature* though.'

Julia was still at a loss to explain the Nottingham and Southampton results and the second mystery person in Oxford. So she asked LJM.

'I don't know who the other person in Oxford is, but my son is at Nottingham University and my eldest daughter is at Southampton University,' he replied.

'What about Exeter?'

'My youngest daughter lives there.'

'So negative mass runs in the family. Are you aliens?' muttered Julia.

'I'm lighter than I was. I'll say that,' LJM said, ignoring her question.

MI5 was faced with a tough choice:

1. Round up all known carriers of negative mass in an attempt to keep a lid on the security aspects.

2. Accept that negative mass may be a naturally occurring phenomenon in people and that this is another form of racism. In this case, letting the people with negative mass go free in the community seems like the right thing to do, except that they may be the target of terrorist attacks.

They decided that the best course of action was the second option. They would let LJM go and not attempt to round up his children. By not taking the matter any further, they were giving them the best chance of not being leaked to a terrorist organisation.

THE USA WEIGHS IN

Having obtained an NM detector made in the UK and then having made one of their own via the Black Obsidian organisation, the USA was up to speed. The only thing they didn't have was someone like LJM in their custody so they could do further experiments on someone carrying negative mass.

They knew all about LJM from the Blue Crystal operation. MI5 hadn't leaked the connection with negative mass, but it didn't take long for the Americans to put two and two together, particularly when he was seen with Henning in Exeter.

They had a choice:

1. Borrow LJM from the UK to assist with operations in the USA.

2. Find their own equivalent of LJM, assuming there was at least one of him/her on mainland USA.

They decided to do both.

The project manager at Black Obsidian, Jack Hardaker, was calling the shots.

'Dawn, it's Jack. We really need LJM in the USA to assist with our investigations. Can you make that happen?' he asked.

'Jack, I'll ask the British, but there's no telling what they'll say,' said Dawn.

'Take him if you have to,' asserted Jack.

* * *

Giles took the request from Dawn and immediately drafted a memo for the prime minister.

Theresa May debated the matter with her adviser.

'I can't just say yes without asking him first. What do the Americans think this is? But if we give him a choice, he may as well say no to us all. He's had his life jerked around that much. Then if we let him go, the Americans will probably kidnap him anyway. I seem to be caught between the devil and the deep blue sea,' she surmised.

'I'd advise that you ask him and then do what he wants. We're on thin ice keeping him in custody anyway. He's done nothing wrong,' he advised.

* * *

Julia approached LJM.

'Bob, that's you name, isn't it? The government wants to thank you for your contributions to the greater good with all the work done so far,' she said.

'No problem,' he responded.

'We wish to let you go from further operations, but the USA has put in a request for you to join them with their investigations.'

'And if I refuse?' he asked.

'Then expect to get bundled into the back of a van,' she replied pointedly.

'OK, I'll do what they want, but leave my children out of it,' he argued irritably.

Next thing, LJM was on a flight to New York. He had virtually no belongings.

'LJM, it's Jack. Pleased to meet you,' said Jack. 'LJM?' queried LJM.

'It's your code name. It means Leather Jacket Man.' 'OK,' said Bob.

'You'll be working with an organisation known as Black Obsidian', said Jack, 'to help us understand the implications of negative mass.'

'Negative mass?' queried LJM.

'The stuff you're carrying that makes you special,' answered Jack.

LJM also considered the coincidence that his story was also named Black Obsidian, but he decided to keep it to himself.

Having LJM in their custody partly assuaged the Americans' thirst for information. But there was no getting away from the fact that what they really wanted to do was to track down every person in the USA who was carrying negative mass.

The procedure for doing that was basically to use the Khan EM machine to follow every minor signal and then use the negative-mass detector to confirm the result. This was essentially Blue Crystal all over again.

The difference was the Americans wanted to track down every city, so this would mean deploying hardware on a massive scale.

Each EM machine would need to be tested in the Nevada desert before it could be put into operation.

The crowd control implications of this were mind-boggling. Every city would be done simultaneously to avoid rumours spreading between operations and things getting out of hand. There would be one big bang evening of hell from the Hum. Then later on would be smaller operations to track down individual signals.

Donald Trump had the memo in his hand. This was the biggest and hottest of hot potatoes in his career.

'I'm not sure about this one. On the one hand, I can understand the security implications of tracking this stuff down. On the other hand is the reality that I will get called a Nazi for conducting an experiment on the American people without their consent,' he mused.

'The decision is yours, Mr President,' advised his advisor.

'To hell with it. Let's do it,' he declared. In one fell swoop, he became technically the most racist president in history.

'Jack, it's Malcolm. The president has signed off on the big bang proposal. The Blue Crystal company will make all of the hardware. Then Black Obsidian will take overall control for managing the ground operation. The military will operate the hardware,' said Malcolm Nuttall.

'Jeepers, I had no idea that he would authorise something like that,' said Jack.

'Me neither,' said Malcolm. 'And I wrote the proposal. I'm more used to writing things that never see the light of day.'

'I'd like to get Kingsley Khan in on this seeing as he's the inventor of the machine,' continued Malcolm.

'Do you want Julia Barnes as well? She was his boss,' asked Jack.

'She's at MI5 now, isn't she?' queried Malcolm. 'They all are,' stated Jack.

'Go on then. See to it that Dawn gets on to it right away,' finished Malcolm.

Giles called a meeting with Julia and the Mongols.

'I'll get right to the point. The USA is embarking on a Blue Crystal–style operation on their mainland. They've requested that Kingsley and Julia be available to assist from their headquarters in New York.'

'Is this a genuine request, or is it the same kind of loaded offer that was made to LJM?' queried Julia.

'They really want you to go,' answered Giles.

Henning in particular was not happy. 'I can't abide this business of experimenting on people without their consent. But I'll watch from afar to support my friends.'

Kingsley agreed.

'Off to America we go,' said Julia.

When they landed in New York, the two of them checked in to the Holiday Inn Express hotel on the grounds it was close to Black Obsidian headquarters in Manhattan.

They both took a moment to admire the Empire State Building. Then Julia took some time on her own to go shopping. 'I may as well now, before it all kicks off big time,' she said.

When she came back, they took time to go to a bar and then have an evening meal out.

'So', he said, 'can I ask you out to the prom?'

'I never went to the school prom. I went to a Catholic school, and my parents were very poor, so they couldn't afford a dress. But I really appreciate being asked.' She smiled.

<hr>

'Julia, it's Jack. We haven't met.'

'Please to meet you.' They shook hands. 'Kingsley, good to meet you again.'

'Jack, I'll get right to the point,' said Julia. 'We've discussed things amongst ourselves, and this whole proposal of experimenting on the population at large without their consent frightens us. We have experience of what the Khan EM machine is like on the ground, and used at high power, it generates the Hum at significant volume and electrocutes people at short range. If you're going to cover an area the size of New York in one hit, the fallout will be terrifying. Quite aside from the ethical dimension if this should ever get out.'

'That's exactly the kind of feedback we need so we can get the best plan,' said Jack.

'I have a suggestion,' said Kingsley. 'If we use multiple smaller machines, we can do the districts of New York with, say, one each.'

'Well said, man,' said Jack.

Julia Skyped Henning and Theo to let them know what was going on.

Jack's responses did little to manage Henning's fears. In particular, he seemed to just translate them into a new version of what was essentially the same plan. What was he expecting? Henning told himself. But the fears didn't go away. They just festered. Henning knew that talking to Julia any further was pointless because she'd given it her best shot with Jack. What to do? He could go over Jack's head and talk to Malcolm, or he could go one further and try to approach the president. He put such thoughts aside for the moment and got out his iPod instead. First up was 'The End' by the Doors.

Kingsley meanwhile was having no such qualms. He'd gone along with Julia's peacekeeping efforts for the sake of keeping the peace but was not particularly bothered himself. As long as they didn't cause an earthquake or kill anyone, then he was fine with it. Speaking of which, it occurred to him that San Francisco was probably on the list of targeted cities, which would mean hitting the San Andreas fault with a good proportion of full power from the EM machine. Not for the faint-hearted. Kingsley listened to music on his phone. He was playing 'Sympathy for the Devil' by the Rolling Stones.

Theo was treading a middle ground. He could understand the concerns but wasn't prepared to make a stand. His choice of music was whatever was going on in his head at the time. He was often found humming and was currently on 'My Way' by Frank Sinatra.

Julia was doing her best to represent the views of her team, but there was no doubt she sympathised with Henning. She had experienced the Hum first-hand and had seen the effects of electrocution close up when the police officer was caught outside the industrial unit in Exeter. Like Kingsley, she was interested to know what would happen to San Andreas. Her choice of music was currently 'California Dreamin'' by Sia.

—∿∿⦿⟨⦾⟩⦿∿∿—

Jack called a meeting with Julia.

'Julia, we've got some progress on the plans. We're looking to target major cities in the hunt for negative mass. The list of cities is as follows: (1) New York, (2) Los Angeles, (3) Chicago, (4) Houston, (5) San Francisco, (6) Washington DC. There are plenty of other cities we could target, but this is the short list for now,' he said. 'I'd like to assign responsibilities for the ground operations in each of these places. I'll take Chicago and Houston. Would you care to choose two of the remainder amongst your team?' he continued.

Julia went pale. Then she composed herself. 'I'll take New York. Kingsley can take San Francisco.'

Basically, Julia was putting herself on the front line in the largest city in the United States with a population of 8 million.

'I want to conduct a test, Jack, in somewhere remote, like the Nevada desert. I want to know what's the lowest power setting we can use for coverage in a given area. I'm also assuming that people in high-rise buildings will be effectively insulated from the bulk of the signal. So you won't get the whole of the population,' she pointed out.

However perturbed his colleagues back in the UK, Kingsley was fine with it.

Interestingly, Julia liked the position of power she was in. So she put her personal feelings aside. She hung on to New York, Kingsley hung on to San Francisco, and she returned DC and Los Angeles to Jack.

It was an open question as to what Henning and Theo were actually going to do. Giles put some thought into it and came up with deputy for Julia and Kingsley, respectively.

Henning still complained and was basically read the riot act by Giles. He left the office fuming.

Henning planned to go back to Exeter but not before he had taken a visit to the *Daily Mail*. Although he'd signed a non-disclosure agreement with MI5, he'd done no such thing with Black Obsidian.

Henning met with Stephanie Francis.

'Henning, it's good to meet you. Can you tell me why you're here?' she asked.

'Recently I worked with a secret US government organisation called Black Obsidian. They are planning on using new physics to experiment on the local population in major cities in the USA without their consent,' he replied.

'Does that include New York?' 'Yes, that's on the list.'

'Do you have the list?'

Henning realised he was toast as far as Jack was concerned.

'New York, Los Angeles, San Francisco, and Washington DC. There are probably others too, but these are the ones I know about,' said Henning.

'This is sensational!' exclaimed Stephanie. 'What about the technology?'

'The relevant technology is something called the electromagnetic or EM machine. It was invented by my friend and colleague Kingsley Khan. At short range, it electrocutes people. At medium range, it stuns them, and at long range, they experience the Hum. As a side effect, it can trigger earthquakes,' he concluded.

'Seriously? They're planning on using it in San Francisco, and it triggers earthquakes? Are they completely mad?' she queried.

'Afraid so. They're doing it because it will give them information on all the people carrying negative mass. That's the other part of the new physics. It's nothing short of racism though,' he expounded.

'Negative mass?' she queried.

'If you imagine a positive mass with a weight of one kilogram, the equivalent negative mass would have a weight of minus one kilogram. Therefore, it would float upwards against the force of gravity. It seems that some people are carrying an amount of it in their bodies,' he explained.

'And the point about racism?'

'If you use a negative-mass detector to track down all people carrying it in their bodies, then you've just implemented another form of racism. The White House will argue that these people constitute a security risk based on fear of the unknown,' he replied.

'And what was your part in all this?'

'I took part in an EM machine operation in Exeter,' finished Henning.

'Thank you, Henning. That will be all for now,' accepted Stephanie.

The *Daily Mail* sold their story to the *New York Times* instead of running with it. The *NYT* attended the next White House press briefing and asked a question at the end.

'Mr President, can you confirm that a secret government organisation called Black Obsidian is planning on experimenting on the local population in major cities across the country?' asked Laura Jones.

'No, that's an unsubstantiated rumour with no basis in fact,' denied Donald Trump.

'Can you at least confirm that Black Obsidian exists?' she continued, sensing that he was lying.

'That's classified,' he rebuffed.

'What about the fact that Kingsley Khan is the inventor of a machine that causes earthquakes and that he's planning on using it in San Francisco?' she persisted.

'That's classified,' he again responded, looking visibly ruffled, conscious that he'd probably given too much away.

'Thank you very much for confirming, Mr President,' she concluded.

As the last remaining Mongol in Thames House, Theo got to attend one of the top-secret meetings at New Age Technologies. In this particular case, they'd developed a body scanner version of the NM detector. As they no longer had LJM in the UK, it was an open question who it could be tested on. Theo arranged with Giles to have one shipped to Black Obsidian so they could test it there.

For the time being, Julia and the remaining Mongols knew nothing of Henning's betrayal. So Julia went right ahead in identifying sites for the New York ground operation. It didn't occur to her that this level of planning was common to terrorism.

Kingsley was booked on a flight to San Francisco. Little did he know that travelling in his own name was a complete no-no from here on.

He arrived at San Francisco International Airport and walked right into the lens of a reporter.

'Kingsley Khan, we hear that you're the inventor of the electromagnetic EM machine. Is it true that you're the first person to trigger an earthquake? What's your business in San Francisco? Are you planning on triggering the San Andreas fault? You're a dangerous man, Kingsley Khan. You're not welcome here.'

'Look, I have absolutely no intention of triggering the San Andreas fault. It's true that I triggered an earthquake in Exeter by operating at full power on Dartmoor which is close by. That's basically a massive granite outcrop with associated magma chamber. I won't be operating in that manner here,' he replied truthfully.

'So what is the purpose of your visit?' 'Sightseeing,' he said ambiguously.

Miraculously, they let Kingsley go about his business. 'Move along, move along.'

Kingsley instantly picked up his phone to call Julia.

'J., it's K. I was rolling along here in San Francisco, and the press ambushed me. They knew my name and all about triggering earthquakes. Has Henning been talking to them?

I'm assuming it wasn't you or Jack who told them,' he said crossly.

'It could be coincidental. The leak could have occurred when we were in Exeter. We tried to keep a lid on everything, but given that an earthquake actually happened, it was bound to get out sooner or later. I have no idea whether Henning leaked anything since his departure,' she replied coolly.

When Julia got off the phone, she sent a memo to Malcolm.

Malcolm's first line of business, however, was to upgrade their negative-mass detector to the latest specifications. This meant being able to measure how much negative mass there was within 25 miles of Manhattan. Like the British, he decided to deploy it as a mobile unit in a van, and they simply parked it close to Ground Zero, letting the police know what they were up to so they wouldn't get arrested. It must have looked mightily suspicious to anyone watching, with something that looked like a bomb being left out in the open. At least the agents were still on hand and hadn't deserted their experiment.

When the result came back, it told them there were minus three kilograms of negative mass in New York. If you counted LJM as minus one and a half, then that left one more person out there.

LJM meanwhile was bored. He'd been lured to the USA on a promise of being needed as a high priority, yet the reality was, apart from a body scanner test, he wasn't needed at all.

He decided to reconnect by visiting Ground Zero for the terrorist attacks on 9/11. He thought he would do his typical prayer stunt where he lay face down on the ground, arms and legs spread wide, and then the same thing but face up.

He wasn't expecting to hear a voice. But he did. Again, it was the voice of a woman.

'Are you Patsy?' he said. 'No, I am Anisa,' she replied.

'Whereabouts on planet Earth are you?' he quizzed. 'Java in Indonesia,' she answered.

'Stay there. I'm coming to get you,' he said boldly. 'And what is your name? she asked.

'Bob,' he replied.

'How will you find me?' 'I trust in the universe.'

LJM went back to Jack and requested a holiday. Given that they weren't in need of his services at that time, this seemed to make sense.

'Where are you going?' asked Jack. 'Indonesia,' replied LJM.

'Off you go. Just make sure you come back here. And take your phone with you,' authorised Jack.

Jack went straight into a meeting with Malcolm.

'LJM has just had a holiday to Indonesia signed off by me,' said Jack.

'It's a marvel how these things work,' said Malcolm. 'Why?' queried Jack.

'Because we've just identified Indonesia as our target foreign country for doing negative-mass experiments,' answered Malcolm.

'Why Indonesia?' asked Jack reasonably.

'We reckon it's impractical to do China, India, or the USA, particularly given the press leaks in our own country. Indonesia is number 4 on the list of populated countries,' reasoned Malcolm.

'So we won't be doing the evening of hell then?' concluded Jack.

'Not here. No, that was bound to leak out at some point. We'll concentrate on New York and possibly San Francisco for the earthquake connection. That should tell us what we need to know,' finalised Malcolm.

Julia was informed of the negative-mass result for New York. That told her that her entire operation was basically to track down one person.

She'd argued with Jack that having mobile Ford Transit SuperVans for the EM operation was preferable to fixed industrial units. That way, she could follow up with repeated measurements to home in on the person concerned. It wasn't a very precise procedure and could easily result in the person getting away. This was the best she could do.

When the time came, eight high-powered SuperVans drove out of the Nevada desert in a variety of colourful liveries. Destination New York, courtesy of Julia.

They were closely followed by another ten high-powered SuperVans, destination Indonesia, courtesy of Jack.

Meanwhile, Kingsley got to take an NM detector to San Francisco. They figured he was much less likely to get stopped by the press if he was driving a van. He pointed out that he'd been robbed twice whilst doing a similar thing in the UK, but Jack and Malcolm were confident that they didn't have that kind of a leak. Yes, Henning had likely spilled the beans, but that was all done and dusted. Kingsley offered the chance to assign a military escort in front and behind, but that was declined on the basis of not wanting to draw attention.

So it was déjà vu all over again. Kingsley took a military transport plane from coast to coast. It was noisy as hell, so he didn't get to hold much in way of conversation.

When he got there, he drove out of the military base into a police checkpoint.

'Kingsley Khan I presume?' ventured the officer. 'Yes, what's this all about?' flustered Kingsley.

'You're being arrested under terrorism laws. Please step out of the van.'

Henning was disappointed the press hadn't gone public with his story and didn't realise the kind of pressure Kingsley was being put under as a result. This wasn't the result he'd hoped for. So he went back to Exeter to focus on his QE machine.

The last thing that had happened on that front was he'd established a hearing-voice connection with LJM. It was only one-way, so Henning couldn't hear LJM, but it was a start. He wondered whether LJM would be able to hear from a long distance away, so he set up his machine on the highest power setting.

He pressed go, and the usual flashes of light and sounds occurred. He then got on the phone with LJM, but by this time, he was on a flight to Jakarta. So with no answer, Henning was left wondering what the results of his experiment really were.

Jack wasn't impressed when he heard that Kingsley had been arrested. He went straight to Malcolm to get him to apply some pressure. When Malcolm got involved though, he ran into some resistance. Being a separate group outside the CIA had its drawbacks. So he escalated, and the president got involved.

After much wrangling, Kingsley was set free. Nobody fancied having the president on terrorism charges, so they got away with it for the time being.

Julia inspected her brand-new SuperVans before giving their drivers and machine operators a briefing. She didn't suspect that the sheer act of doing so put the whole operation under much more threat of compromise, but in the event, she got away with it. The vans weren't spotted because nobody saw them coming. Julia had been very economical with whom she'd told about it all. Basically, she and Jack were the only ones.

'Thank you all for driving from Nevada. This is a historic operation. New York will be a safer place once we have the information from this evening. Here are the destinations. Please drive directly to your destination and be ready to go with the experiment at precisely 7 p.m. Then depending on the results, you all need to be ready to go for one or more follow-up operations,' she commanded.

The SuperVans drove out to their allotted initial destinations in the districts of New York. In rough terms, this meant each van covering about one million people.

When the time came, they each pressed Go. As these were uprated high-power SuperVans, their impact on the local environment was significant.

Julia could instantly hear it as the Hum and assumed that most of New York could too. This was the bit she didn't like. Real people were being affected and would likely be bringing out the placards the next day.

Several people were caught up close to the vans in a dance of electrocution. If Julia was lucky, there would be no deaths, but there was no guarantee. At least the vans were lower in power than the industrial unit version.

Then she remembered the security guards in Exeter who did lose their lives. They might have recovered if they hadn't been shot dead on Jack's orders. She would be giving no such orders today. She told herself that she wasn't really Darth Vader, but the reality was, she was taking a hell or a risk with people's lives. If anyone did die on her command, then she would be subject to antiterrorism laws herself.

Black Obsidian was appropriate in more ways than one. The colour black admirably described the connection with evil.

Julia received the results from the first round. It showed a major signal in the direction of the UK, which was to be expected. Then there was a significant minor signal in the Bronx district. She deployed all eight SuperVans in random locations in the Bronx and gave an allotted time.

This process was repeated three times until she had a fix on a particular building close to the county courthouse. Given a list of people inside it would be a simple process to round them up and test for negative mass, given a sensitive enough detector.

The next day, the *New York Times* had done its research and led the front page story with 'The Hum Comes to NY'. It finished with a call for the death penalty for the government officials in charge. They wanted heads on spikes.

Julia went pale in her own distinctive fashion when she read the news. She'd been lucky that nobody actually died, but the rumours of electrocution were rife amongst the local population.

When she went outside for some fresh air, Julia was accosted by a reporter.

'Ms Julia Barnes I presume? I'm Laura Jones from the *New York Times*.'

'Pleased to meet you, Laura. How can I help?' she asked.

Julia's training inclined her to be as nice as possible at the start and then answer 'That's classified' to everything else. But she was in a quandary here. Her path had brought her to this point, and she'd achieved her objective. She almost didn't care what happened from here on. Her heart told her to say 'F— it' and go and do what Henning did.

'We have reason to believe you were in charge of last night's operation to bring the Hum to New York and the Bronx. Is that correct?' queried Laura.

There was a considerable pause.

'Yes, that's right.' Julia felt a huge wave of emotion wash over her. Now to face the music.

'Miss, I recommend taking you to the office of the *New York Times*. It isn't safe for you here.'

'OK.'

They got there without incident, and she negotiated a price for her story before she spilled the beans. Julia faced an extraordinarily thorough debrief. She was honest about her roles in the CIA and MI5 and then Black Obsidian. She named Jack and Malcolm but stopped short of naming the president as the next in the chain of command. The press were on to that thanks to Henning.

Once the debrief was over, three police officers turned up for Julia.

'This wasn't part of the deal!' she exclaimed. 'No, but it's a major part of the story.'

'Ms Barnes, you're under arrest for bringing terror to New York. You have the right to remain silent. Anything you do say may be taken down in evidence and used in a court of law.'

Julia knew this was serious. She couldn't expect any assistance from Malcolm in getting her out. On terrorism charges, she could expect to spend the rest of her time in a supermax prison. She was taken away in handcuffs.

What Julia hadn't bargained on was how things would appear to Jack and Malcolm. The most likely interpretation was that Julia had been arrested and then sold her story to the press, not the other way around. Although they weren't best pleased, they were a lot happier than in Henning's case. So Malcolm made an attempt to intervene on Julia's behalf. However, he ran into much more resistance than he had with Kingsley's case. After all, she had been caught, more or less, red-handed.

So the issue came to rest with the president. If he was prepared to declare his support for Black Obsidian, then that could be enough to get her off the hook. If not, then she faced a bleak future. Of course, he denied any involvement. So that left Malcolm and Jack squarely in the frame.

The police had subpoenaed Julia's testimony to the *New York Times*, and so they were aware of her references to Jack Hardaker and Malcolm Nuttall. It should have been a simple matter to get her to confirm their identity, but she was playing hardball, so she clammed up.

Before long, the police had a warrant to search the Black Obsidian premises. There they found enough to put Jack and Malcolm away. They were soon arrested and were behind bars.

The *New York Times* took their cue and published Julia's story. 'Terrorist Cell Black Obsidian in Police Custody' ran the headline.

Kingsley was reading a copy as the most senior person left in the office. He passed it on to Theo when he was done.

'Kingsley, should we even be coming into work now that our bosses have been arrested?' asked Theo.

'Probably not. I'll stay here long enough to see if I can get an audience with the president. Then I'll phone Giles. Then I'll go and see Julia,' replied Kingsley.

Kingsley was as good as his word. But the president wasn't as good as his. He both refused a meeting and threatened to expose Kingsley as a member of Black Obsidian.

He phoned Giles, but Giles was out to lunch—such was the time difference between New York and London. So he went one better and phoned his counterpart in the USA, Dawn Deacon. However, Dawn was evasive and not much help. Little did Kingsley know that she had been the source of some of the leaks earlier on in the project.

He and Theo then went in search of whatever was the closest vehicle at hand and came up with a SuperVan.

'Poetic indeed,' he muttered under his breath.

Kingsley knew that the consequences for being caught would be severe given the current climate. But something emboldened him, and he wasn't scared of arrest in the event he was able to drive to the police station without incident.

'I'm Kingsley Khan, and this is Theofanes Raptor, both here to see Julia Barnes.'

'I'm afraid we don't allow visitors. You'll be able to visit her when she's in prison,' came the curt reply.

Kingsley remembered that Julia had posed as his lawyer when the roles were reversed. He wasn't able to do that for her, particularly now that his cover was blown. He took a moment to chew the cud and decide what to do next. For a moment, he debated whether putting the SuperVan into action and electrocuting everyone in the police station was a good idea but decided he wasn't actually a terrorist, so he wouldn't be going down that road. Then it came to him that exposing the operation as led by the president was the way out of the bind. There would be evidence elsewhere in the USA for the commissioning of the SuperVans for example.

Once Kingsley had made up his mind, there was no stopping him.

'Come on, Theo. We're going to the *New York Post*.'
'If you say so, boss,' replied Theo.

Once there, Kingsley got out of the SuperVan and went inside to find someone from the *New York Post* who would deal with his story.

'I'm Kingsley Khan, inventor of the EM machine that was used to electrocute people and deliver the Hum to millions of people yesterday. This is a SuperVan, a mobile version of the EM machine, though it used to be a QE machine as well.'

There was a palpable look of terror in the eyes of the people listening.

'Well, do you want my story or not?' hissed Kingsley irritably. 'Do you have an appointment?' came the timid reply.

'I don't need an appointment when I'm sitting on the biggest story in the history of this newspaper,' fumed Kingsley.

'Right you are. I'll get someone,' promised the timid one.

'Kingsley, this is Marion Lambert from the *New York Post*. Before we begin, can you confirm whether you were part of the operation on Monday?' she asked.

'No, I wasn't,' he replied, much calmer now. 'I am the inventor of the machine that was used in the operation, but this is old technology now. It's been in service for a number of years.'

Kingsley went on to give her a full rundown of the SuperVan and its capabilities.

'I can give you a demo if you wish.' He grinned. '*No! That won't be necessary.*' She looked horrified.

'The point behind all this is that it's been reported in the *New York Times* that Black Obsidian is a terror cell operating on US soil. Yet the reality is that it's been very much a part of the US government, and the man in charge, Malcolm Nuttall, reported directly to the president. He can't just deny that now the heat has been turned up. If you dig deep, you'll find marks of the USA everywhere, including this SuperVan, which was made in Nevada,' reasoned Kingsley.

'I think we should surrender the SuperVan as evidence to the police,' suggested Marion.

'Why don't the *New York Post* keep it for now, and I'll lead the police to where the rest of them are being held,' bargained Kingsley.

With that, the police turned up in force—three sets of blue flashing lights.

'Kingsley Khan, you're under arrest for suspected terrorism,' asserted the officer.

'Well, I have to say it's about time. But you're missing the point, you muppets. I can show you where many tons of evidence are being stored,' pushed Kingsley.

The police debated what to do and decided to take Kingsley at his word and drive to Black Obsidian central.

LJM landed at Jakarta airport and caught a cab into the centre of the city. How to find someone in the middle of such a big metropolis with five million people? He was convinced that he was in the right place already, so no need to search the rest of Java.

He felt an urge and decided to seek out a brothel. Predictably, he ended up in the red-light district.

No, he didn't want to be licked from head to toe; he was looking for someone called Anisa. But no luck.

So he checked in to the Best Western Hariston Hotel and waited for morning.

When he got up for breakfast, he went out of his room on the ground floor and into the corridor. A chambermaid was pushing a trolley full of towels.

'Are you Anisa?' he asked.

'Yes,' she said excitedly. 'Are you Bob?'

'Yes, I am,' said LJM. 'Also known as Leather Jacket Man, or LJM, according to the Yanks.'

'How did you find me?'

'I would say it was pure luck, but I know the universe better than that.'

The next thing that happened was that both LJM and Anisa went into a series of convulsions from electrocution. It lasted for several minutes.

When it finished, LJM came up for air.

'That was the Yanks too. They're searching for you. I have enough money for a plane ticket to get you out of here. Let's go,' he said grimly.

'Why are they searching for me?' she asked almost hysterically.

'It's to do with something called negative mass. You're carrying some of it in your body, and that's what makes you telepathic. They want to round you up so they can conduct experiments on you. That's what they've been doing with me,' he explained.

'How did you get away?' she quizzed.

'I took a holiday,' he replied truthfully. 'They trust me.'

'OK, I will go with you,' declared Anisa, excited to be going on an adventure. 'Where are we going?'

'Australia.'

At that point, LJM heard Henning's voice in his head.

'LJM, you're needed here in the UK. Please make your way here as soon as you're done with your holiday in Indonesia,' said Henning.

'I'm going to Australia first, but yes, I'll head to the UK after that,' replied LJM, hopeful that the response would get through.

'Ah, the marvels of modern technology!' he exclaimed. 'Who was that?' she asked.

'Henning in the UK,' he replied.

'Wow, you really are telepathic, aren't you?' she marvelled.

'Sometimes it works naturally, and sometimes it works with technological assistance. I haven't got it totally figured out. Lying on the ground spread-eagled seems to help.'

When Kingsley got to Black Obsidian headquarters courtesy of the police, he wasted no time in showing them the fleet of SuperVans.

'That's very helpful, but you're still under arrest.'

With Julia, Kingsley, Jack, and Malcolm behind bars, the federal agents had done a good job of getting Black Obsidian off the streets. They decided not to pursue the SuperVan drivers and operators, who were believed to be military in origin, but they couldn't prove that.

However, the company that made the SuperVans, Blue Crystal, remained uncompromised. So it was still a mystery where the SuperVans came from, though the rumour was that they were home-grown in the USA.

With the identity of Blue Crystal withheld, it was an easy matter for the president to deny any involvement with Black Obsidian. This message got through to Henning.

Henning decided he would offer himself as a witness to try and break the deadlock. This was to help Julia and Kingsley. He didn't much care for Jack and Malcolm but realised they would probably be released too if his plan worked. It did mean breaking the terms of his original agreement with Blue Crystal, but to hell with it. It was worth it to free his friends.

LJM and Anisa flew to Alice Springs, Australia. 'Who are we going to pick up?' queried Anisa.

'Patsy. She's another telepathic like you. I contacted her from Exeter last year, whereas I contacted you from New York this year,' he explained.

'How do you know she'll even be here?' she quizzed. 'I trust in the universe,' he responded cryptically. 'Where are we going after this?' she continued.

'Exeter. To meet the members of my family. I think they're all like us,' he explained.

'Do they all live in Exeter?'

'They'll all be down for a family reunion.'

When they got to the bar he'd met Patsy in before, it was deserted.

'OK, I'm wrong. I'm going to have to ask a question.'

He lay down on the ground, face down, arms and leg apart. 'Patsy, can you hear me?' he shouted.

'Of course, I can. I'm right here.' She grinned. LJM looked up to see Patsy standing above him.

'I've seen you coming. I thought I'd play a simple trick on you,' she added.

'We have to go. And you're coming with us,' he said directly. 'Have I got a chance to pack a bag?'

'So you didn't see that coming?'

When they arrived at Heathrow, LJM, Anisa, and Patsy caught a flight to Exeter. LJM phoned ahead to arrange with his son and two daughters to meet at Goa Spice.

His eldest daughter drove the other two in her blue BMW Mini with Union Jack on the roof. LJM and the other two arrived by taxi.

The weather was getting particularly stormy.

They all went inside to sit down. LJM made the introductions. He introduced Anisa and Patsy as his two girlfriends.

A tornado touched down in the St Thomas churchyard just outside.

Once the meal was over, LJM contacted Henning and convinced his children that they should make an urgent visit to the Begbroke Science Park in Oxford where a negative-mass detector was waiting. He told Anisa and Patsy to wait here whilst he hired a car from Marsh Barton.

They drove in convoy along the A303 and up the A34.

When they got to the Begbroke Science Park, Henning and Theo were waiting. Henning explained that they had the latest version of the body scanner, which was sensitive to individual body parts. Theo took the details of everyone present.

They took turns in the body scanner. First Harriet, then Alex, Esther, Anisa, Patsy, and then finally, LJM.

Then there was a short wait for the results.

'You've all tested positive for negative mass,' announced Henning.

'And you're all showing minus one and a half kilograms in your liver. That makes you three kilograms lighter than you would expect,' added Theo.

'That explains it,' said LJM.

Back outside, they had to run to their cars because of the stormy weather. LJM clocked what was going on and suggested to his eldest daughter that they drive back separately.

Theo also clocked what was going on and concluded that the Oxford ring road winds were reality rather than myth.

LJM's adventure with Anisa and Patsy continued when they returned to Exeter, dropped off the car, got a taxi to Exeter airport, and caught a flight back to Heathrow.

'I promised to return to New York, so we'll do that next,' he proposed.

Henning's testimony to the Supreme Court proved crucial. He dug out the original QE machine contract between him and Blue Crystal as evidence that the company was real and based in the USA. He pointed out that Kingsley would have done a similar thing for the EM machine, which went on to be the basis of SuperVan. Julia's testimony that the drivers and operators were military and Malcolm's testimony that the president ordered Black Obsidian were enough to impeach the president on terrorism charges.

Malcolm, Jack, Julia, and Kingsley were set free. They returned to their office at just the time that LJM turned up with Anisa and Patsy.

'LJM, good to meet you again. How was the holiday? And who are these two young ladies you have with you?' asked Jack.

'Fine, apart from being electrocuted. This is Anisa, and she's telepathic. And this is Patsy, and she's telepathic and can see into the future. We're all carrying negative mass. We had it confirmed by the British,' responded LJM pointedly.

'Ah, I see. Would you care to take the body scanner test again just to show us what you say is indeed fact?'

'Fine.'

When the results came back, they showed all three carrying negative mass.

'You are very valuable people. Thanks for making the trip here,' said Malcolm.

'I heard you were tracking down more of us in New York,' said LJM.

'It turned out to be just one person, but we never found them,' said Jack.

'I'll find him or her for you,' offered LJM. 'Seriously? How will you do that?' asked Julia. 'I trust in the universe,' said LJM.

'Well, OK, that would be very helpful,' finalised Malcolm incredulously.

⁓ₒₒₑₜₒₒₜₑₒₒ⁓

LJM went back to Central Park, with Anisa and Patsy. Together they lay on the ground face up.

'Do you hear anyone?' asked LJM.

'Yes, I've got someone called Shanice in the Bronx,' said Patsy.

'Me too,' added Anisa.

'OK, that's good enough for me,' said LJM.

They caught a cab to the Bronx and directed the driver to the county courthouse.

When they got there, Shanice was waiting for them on the pavement.

'No messing around?' said LJM.

'No, I thought I'd show you how to see into the future properly.' She grinned.

She squeezed into the back of the cab with Anisa and Patsy, and together they made their way back to Black Obsidian.

BLACK OPERATIONS

Predictably, Shanice passed the test for negative mass.

'So there you have the results of your search for people. Are you satisfied now?' asked LJM rhetorically.

'I can see we'd have been accused of racism hunting for a black woman,' said Julia.

'You'd be accused of racism just trying to track down negative mass, white bitch,' countered Shanice.

'Steady on. There's no need to call anyone a black or white bitch,' cautioned LJM.

It occurred to LJM that he seemed to be building up a bit of a harem, what with Anisa, Patsy, and Shanice all turning out to be women. He needed a different strategy to find men. Perhaps the way to do that was to leave it to the women. They could build up a network of contacts, a bit like he had done, and so on until everyone with negative-mass telepathy had been found out.

Outside, the weather was building up into a storm.

⬥

With Black Obsidian reforming, Malcolm called a meeting to include Jack, Julia, and Kingsley.

'People, we have a complex situation. The president faces terrorism charges, so he will argue that the nation faced an unknown threat from negative mass. This will effectively make the whole thing public knowledge. We've been prevented legally from ever using the EM machine again in peacetime, but it opens up the way for it to be used as a weapon of war. LJM has effectively done our work for us by tracking down Shanice. It seems that he uses telepathy to get in contact with other carriers of negative mass. Once found, they can also display other parapsychological effects, such as seeing the future. We've learnt from the British that all subjects tested thus far have minus one and a half kilograms of negative mass in their liver. This seems to make them three kilograms lighter than would otherwise be,' elaborated Malcolm.

'Can we leave it up to LJM and his harem to track down other carriers? We'd just have to pay for plane tickets, and then they could arrive back here of their own accord. That's a perfect situation to manage because it manages itself,' suggested Kingsley.

'Theo has reported a possible weather connection when carriers are concentrated into a small area. There were storms in Oxford and apparently a tornado in Exeter. This also tallies with a conspiracy theory noted by Theo and myself when we originally visited Oxford and observed clockwise winds on the ring road,' said Julia.

'Well, it's stormy outside. And we have four carriers in here. Presumably, all this hinges on the negative-mass component in their liver. What would it be worth to convince a carrier to have a liver transplant so we would have a specimen to work with?' postulated Jack.

'That's gross,' said Henning, via teleconference, knowing full well that his views would be ignored.

'We have another three confirmed carriers in the UK and a further unconfirmed carrier in Oxford. Perhaps Black Obsidian would do well to repeat the methodology in the USA. Basically, you just use the advanced NM detector that tells you how much negative mass is within a given radius. That would generate a list of unconfirmed carriers by location to pass to LJM and his team. The last I heard, there was no embargo on using the NM detector, so this should be fine,' proposed Theo.

'Well done, team,' responded Malcolm. 'We've got enough ideas here to move forward.'

Malcolm had a meeting with Jack, Jack had a meeting with Julia, and Julia had a meeting with LJM.

'We're prepared to offer you a million dollars in return for a liver transplant,' she offered.

'That seems cheap. I was thinking more along the lines of a billion pounds,' replied LJM.

'It might seem cheap to you, but we're extending the offer to your harem—I mean team—so if anyone with a positive detection for negative mass wants to take up the offer, they can.'

'How do we know that it won't kill us? I take it you're giving us a normal positive-mass liver as a replacement?' he worried.

'We don't know for certain, hence the high price tag,' she pointed out.

'So it's like Russian roulette.'

'Think of it as advancing medical science.'

LJM toyed with the idea but concluded that with a family, he had too much to lose.

'It's a no from me. I'll have to ask my team.'

When LJM asked Anisa, Patsy, and Shanice, they were predictably horrified.

'This basically puts a price on our heads,' complained Shanice.

Patsy was just as militant. Anisa was the only one to show any sign of softening.

'A million dollars goes a long way where I come from,' declared Anisa.

'You'd have to put up with immunosuppressant medication. That's assuming you survive,' cautioned Patsy.

'It's still a good deal,' insisted Anisa.

'Well, if you're prepared to take one for the team, then it takes the pressure off us,' said LJM. He reported back to Julia that they had a willing candidate.

The operation was scheduled immediately at the New York– Presbyterian Lower Manhattan Hospital.

The procedure was to put Anisa and the replacement liver through the NM body scanner separately first, perform the operation, then put Anisa and her original liver through the scanner separately last.

LJM performed the role of minister for Anisa. 'Do you believe in God?' he asked.

'I do,' she agreed.

'Well, you're in the hands of God for this operation. We pray that he is merciful and will send you back to us alive. Amen.'

'Amen.'

Anisa was due for an overnight stay, followed by two hours of anaesthesia in the morning, and then a four-to-eight-hour operation.

LJM, Patsy, and Shanice left her at the end of visiting time.

The operation did not go well. Anisa rejected the new liver, and the medication was insufficient to supress the immune response. She died on the operating table after five hours, but not until after her old liver was observed floating to the ceiling.

Also, they were able to carry out the NM body scanner tests. These proved that the liver was the source of negative mass, and Anisa's body tested negative for negative-mass post-operation.

The sad news had a profound effect on LJM. He realised that the price on their head would increase now that wacky new macroscopic physics had been discovered. He went into a sharp decline, and with the onset of depression, he asked to go back to the UK. He agreed with Jack that Black Obsidian should settle the bill for plane tickets for himself and Patsy, leaving Shanice to make her own decisions in New York.

Patsy decided to stay in New York, and this meant she effectively took on LJM's role as strongest receiver. Shanice had seen enough and went back to the Bronx.

'Patsy, you're unofficially the most valuable woman in the world,' said Jack.

'I'm aware there is a price on my head—wanted dead and not so bothered about being alive,' she responded.

'We'd prefer it if you could focus on being alive. Can you get in touch with other carriers as LJM got in contact with you?' Jack pushed.

'What, so that they can take the million-dollar challenge and see if they can beat death?' she retorted.

'We won't be doing that again,' said Jack.

'No? What about the black market where they harvest human organs? The unofficial price ticket remains high,' she said pointedly.

'I'm sorry we had to bring all this on you. The black market shouldn't form for as long as the results remain top secret,' he pointed out.

'That isn't very reassuring,' said Patsy.

LJM was in a black mood. He'd gone back to his mother's place in Exeter for a while, but it did little to lift his spirits. He did receive another telepathy call from Henning, asking him to visit Thames House, so he did.

'Why so glum?' asked Henning.

'We lost Anisa in a high-price-tag operation to take her liver. If this is the shape of things to come, then all of us negative- massers can expect a grisly death in the hands of the black market.'

'I'd say listen to some music to cheer you up,' said Henning, offering his iPod.

'Mambo Number 5. / A little bit of Monica in my life. / A little bit of Erica by my side.'

'Weren't you better when you had several women in your life?' quizzed Theo.

'I guess I was,' admitted LJM.

'Well, you're probably missing your friends as much as anything,' said Henning, taking the therapist's role.

'Did you have something you wanted to say to me?' asked LJM.

'Yes, we wanted to reassure you that finding more carriers of negative mass is in the best interests of everyone. The price on your head remains high whilst there aren't very many of you. It would do you some good to lower that as much as you can,' explained Giles.

'So this is basically racism on a grand scale,' countered LJM.

'It's about knowledge—knowledge of who the carriers are so we can all help to keep the black market at bay,' continued Giles. 'You've already found three people for us. Why not carry on and find some more? We'll pay a salary and expenses so you can hop off around the globe whenever you feel like it. Henning and Theo will accompany you so we can observe what decisions you make and why. Basically, we're trying to get a handle on how the telepathy works.'

'Sounds like a dream job in a way,' mused LJM. 'I hope the mood lifts,' finished Giles.

'Thank you, sir,' acknowledged LJM.

'So what's the first destination if we're going to track down some more carriers?' asked Henning.

'Exeter, where I found the old blind seal on the riverbank,' answered LJM.

'Is that where you first contacted Patsy?' asked Theo. 'Yes, it is,' confirmed LJM.

'In that case, we need to disentangle the place from the recipient. How do you know you won't just get in touch with Patsy again?' quizzed Henning.

'Because the universe doesn't seem to work that way,' revealed LJM.

Patsy, for her part, was missing LJM. She looked into the future but saw nothing. So she resorted to going out into Central Park and lying down face up on the ground as if praying to the gods.

'Bob, are you there?'

LJM was missing Patsy too, so she was also on his mind. He'd made the journey to Exeter with Henning and Theo. Then they went to Topsham and walked up the riverbank to where he'd seen the seal. He was now lying face down in his prayer position.

'Patsy are you there?'

'Is that Leather Jacket Man?' Only LJM could hear this. 'Otherwise known as Bob, yes.'

'I was told to expect you.' 'But you're not Patsy?' 'No, I am Geraldine.'

'More women,' muttered LJM under his breath. 'Henning and Theo, I've got someone called Geraldine.'

'Where are you, Geraldine?' 'In Guatemala.'

'OK, I'm coming to get you,' said LJM out loud. 'Boys, it looks like we're going to Guatemala.'

'Before we go to Guatemala, I'd like to check something first. Can we make our way to St Thomas churchyard and then attempt to do a telepathy call from there?'

'I guess, seeing as we're in Exeter,' agreed LJM. 'Who do you expect me to find?'

'We can start by talking to each other. I'll be at Wonford House,' said Henning. Theo went with Henning with the idea of both of them attempting to communicate with LJM.

LJM meanwhile went to St Thomas churchyard. He was left disappointed he hadn't actually managed to speak to Patsy. Oh well. He picked up his phone and called her instead!

'Patsy, it's Bob. How are you?'

'All the better for speaking to you,' replied Patsy.

'I never had the chance to explain what happened to me. You know I'm divorced from Sue?' he said truthfully.

'I gathered that. The question is, are you over it?' she pointed out.

'Enough to want you,' he laid it out there.

'Well, how about you turn up in my life on your own? The last two times, you had other women in tow,' she ruled.

LJM did a quiet cheering gesture because Patsy didn't say no. 'I'll write you some poetry,' he offered as a platitude.

'Poetry? What am I going to do with that?' she said, rejecting the idea.

'OK, OK, I'll find some other way of making it up to you. I'm supposed to go to Guatemala first to pick up another woman. I'll put that on hold and come to see you first,' he said.

'So is this your job now? Picking up women?' she said.

'I'd get in contact with men if I knew how. They just seem to be all women at the moment. There are two scientists here called Henning and Theo who are trying to understand how telepathy works. They'll be going with me,' he said.

'Well, that's a better arrangement. Me too on the job front. They want me to pick up men because they think you'll always get women. But the reality is, I had the telepathic connection with Shanice, not you. So how do you explain that?' she replied.

'Perhaps you're bisexual at heart?' wondered LJM. 'Whereas you're 100 per cent straight?' insinuated Patsy. 'OK, that's enough for now,' said LJM and hung up the call.

He then went back to the business of the telepathy call from Henning and Theo. He waited until he heard something. He said 'I'm ready now' out loud, but still nothing. So he picked up the phone and called Henning.

'Are you trying to contact me?' he asked.

'We'll do it now. Put the phone down,' said Henning.

He heard both Henning's and Theo's voices. Theo said, 'LJM, it's Theo.' And Henning said, 'LJM, it's Henning.'

LJM said 'Pleased to meet you, Theo' and 'Pleased to meet you, Henning' in response.

Then he got back on the phone. 'Anything?' asked LJM. 'Nothing. Did you get our messages?' answered Henning. 'Yes, I got both of them from you and Theo,' responded LJM.

'How about you do a telepathy call from here and let me know if you find anyone?' asked Henning.

LJM tried, but for the first time, he didn't find anyone. He was doing all the praying gestures, but still nothing. 'Perhaps something has got in the way,' he mused to himself. His mind was with Patsy, and the last person he'd contacted was Geraldine. Perhaps the conflict was upsetting things in telepathy land.

Henning noted the failure to telepath and wondered whether LJM could only do one person at a time. Having contacted Geraldine, he needed to finish with her before trying to establish a new connection. It was a theory.

LJM was as good as his word and flew to New York to meet Patsy. The trouble was, he couldn't find her when he got there. It was almost as if his powers had evaporated.

In the end, they did meet up when Patsy returned to the office.

'I didn't see you coming,' she opened. 'I'm a bit off colour,' he countered.

'Why should that affect anything?' she quizzed.

'I don't know. All I know is I tried to telepath, and it didn't work either for the first time since I contacted you.'

'This is a problem because it's affecting me too. What have you done?'

'Nothing. Although I did receive an artificial telepathy call from Henning. That's never upset things in the past.'

'Well, I fell in love with the wizard of telepathy. You'd better get it back if you want me to go with you,' she said harshly.

⚬⚬⚬

Since LJM had his marching orders from Patsy, he decided there was nothing better to do than go and find Geraldine. For the first time, there was a nagging doubt in his mind. What if he couldn't find her? Did he still trust in the universe?

He needn't have worried. Although he had Henning and Theo in tow, he still had the ability to track down a carrier with seemingly effortless ease. In this case, all he did was get off the plane in Guatemala City, and Geraldine was waiting for him on the other side of Customs.

'How did you know when to be here?' asked Henning. 'I didn't know. Just call it inspiration,' said Geraldine. 'Can I be terribly bold?' asked LJM.

'Go on,' said Geraldine. 'We're meant to be lovers.'

Geraldine blushed. 'We've only just met.'

'Well, that's one theory dispensed with,' said Theo. 'What are we doing now that we're here?' asked LJM.

'How about you do a telepathy call and see if anyone comes up this time?' suggested Henning.

So LJM did his spread-eagled stunt in the middle of the arrival hall in the airport. It was noisy, so it was not a location he would otherwise have chosen.

He got nothing.

'I think it could be that it doesn't work when the request comes from us,' said Henning. 'How about you make your own decisions when and where you want to make a call, and we'll just tag along.'

'OK, I'll go with that. Right now, I feel like going back to Patsy in New York. We can also put Geraldine through the NM body scanner.'

'*Ask* Geraldine, not *put*,' emphasised Geraldine.

'Yes, of course,' said LJM apologetically, feeling the pressure from his woman.

When he got to New York, LJM found Patsy waiting for him. 'I saw you propose to Geraldine,' she fumed.

'I'm not one to put it about for real,' he defended. 'Did I try it on with you?'

'You were married at the time,' she sparked.

'I was the first time, but not the second,' he quibbled.

'And then you were with Anisa. How do I know whether you tried it on with her or not?'

'Because I didn't. Anisa was half my age for goodness' sake. And now she's no longer with us. Bless her.'

'This bickering is pointless.' 'You started it.'

'No, I didn't.'

'Yes, you did. You invaded Poland.' Stalemate.

'You know I love you really,' offered LJM.

'But there's always some ulterior motive to your visit. This time, you brought Geraldine to use the NM body scanner. And how do I know it was your telepathy skill working and not hers because you met at the airport?' complained Patsy.

'If you believe I have no skill, then I have no skill. There will always be an alternative explanation,' theorised LJM.

'I want to trust you, but I'm not sure that I do,' said Patsy.

'Then I'm not sure you've fallen in love with me. Not really,' said LJM.

And so they left it.

LJM was free to go and do whatever he wanted, which Henning believed was the secret to his telepathic powers. He would most likely go back to the UK for a bit.

Meanwhile, Patsy was also free to do as she pleased. She'd agreed with Julia that she and Kingsley could monitor what she was doing in much the same way as Henning and Theo were doing with LJM.

The trouble was she had little idea how to initiate a telepathy call. Although she'd accompanied LJM to Central Park, she felt like she was part of his call, not the other way round.

Patsy tried to recreate the circumstances of her first call with LJM, where she was sitting in a car with music playing, but to no avail. She tried being spread-eagled in Central Park, but to no avail either.

'Stretch out with your feelings,' she told herself, remembering the line from Star Wars.

She decided she would visit Ground Zero. And she wouldn't do the spread-eagled thing. She would just sit on her ass, and if that wasn't good enough, then to hell with it.

'How will we know if it's working?' asked Julia. 'I'll start talking to myself,' replied Patsy.

'I'll record your half of the conversation,' said Kingsley optimistically.

'I'm getting something.'

'Pleased to meet you, Derek. I'm Patsy. . . . Yes In New York. . . . Ground Zero. . . . And whereabouts are you? . . . Boulder, Colorado? . . . I'll give you an address. I want you to come visit me here in New York. Is that OK? . . . Bye.'

Patsy's style was different—more controlling than LJM's, but just as effective.

LIVER DISSECTION

Before they went back to the UK, Henning and Theo attended a round-table meeting with Malcolm, Jack, Julia, and Kingsley. Henning opened the batting.

'We've been following LJM around, and he continues to be able to make telepathy calls and meet people in the middle of nowhere. He did have one patch where it didn't seem to be working for him, but we put that down to him following our orders rather than doing what he really wanted. We continue to be able to make artificial telepathy calls via the QE machine, but whilst LJM can hear us, we can't hear him,' reported Henning.

'I suggest you invite Patsy to the UK to see how she does with the QE machine. And whilst you're at it, invite Geraldine as well,' suggested Malcolm. 'That's right. We have a new verified carrier of negative mass.'

There was cheering.

'We've been following Patsy only recently, but she was able to establish a telepathy call with someone called Derek from Boulder, Colorado. At least we assume it's the real thing and she wasn't just making it up. Patsy won't be going to pick him up. He'll be travelling here instead,' reported Julia.

'I can report on the situation with the deceased Anisa. Her liver is continuing to show unusual properties, although as it dries out, its mass is decreasing. Principally it's showing negative-mass symptoms by floating to the ceiling. This makes it officially more valuable than moon rock, in spite of the fact that there seems to be a supply of it in the living population. Her liver will be dissected for further study. It will be cut in half, and then one-half will be kept whole, whilst the other half will be dissected into centimetre cubes. These will be shipped to laboratories around the world for further study. The scientific output from this is immense, and we can expect to dominate the literature for some time,' reported Jack.

'On the weather front, we haven't observed any more tornadoes, but then we haven't had a concentration of carriers like we did before, like six. All I can say is that the weather right now is rainy, and there are four carriers in here. Not conclusive. Perhaps we could arrange for all carriers to meet up specifically so we can measure the weather? We could alert weather stations and get them all on the lookout for something unusual,' reported Theo.

'I'm the only one who doesn't have anything to report. The EM machine is now banned in America. But it isn't banned elsewhere. The obvious thing for me to do is return to the UK and pick up operations there,' reported Kingsley.

'Now we will open the doors and hear from the negative-mass carriers,' announced Malcolm.

LJM, Patsy, Geraldine, and Shanice walked in. There was cheering.

'Anisa is in our thoughts. Perhaps she had to die so that we could live. I take it there's no way you can bring her back to life?' said LJM.

'Afraid not. She's gone, LJM,' ruled Jack.

'Her funeral will be tomorrow. I hope you can all make it,' said Malcolm.

There was a unanimous yes from around the table. 'Well, I hope you're not going to dissect me,' said LJM.

'You're too valuable alive. You all are. Quite apart from the ethical dimension of it,' reassured Malcolm.

'The next trip is to the UK, where Patsy, Shanice, and Geraldine can take the QE machine artificial telepathy challenge. This will establish you as receivers, hopefully, and test you as senders as well. We will require you to undertake a full psychiatric evaluation. I hope this is OK with you,' explained Julia.

'It would also be a good opportunity to take a weather test. If LJM can arrange it with his children, that will be seven carriers all in one place,' said Theo.

'What about Derek?' asked Patsy.

'We'll alert you as and when he shows up,' said Jack.

'The real news of the day is that the president will be set free from terrorism charges on the condition that he doesn't authorise the EM machine on US soil again. And the press will make negative mass fully known to the public, including the identity of known carriers. This means you're all going to be celebrities,' said Kingsley.

'It also means you'll be given secret service protection wherever you go. Don't worry. You'll get used to it. It will be a bit like being the royal family,' said Henning.

'All of this will be a massive distraction. How am I supposed to concentrate on telepathy?' complained LJM.

'I'm confident that you'll find a way,' reassured Henning.

They all attended Anisa's funeral, and this time, it was in the public eye. There were press reporters and TV cameras waiting outside.

'LJM, that's your name, isn't it?'

'My real name is Bob. LJM is my code name,' said LJM.

'Very interesting. Can you confirm that you're the first person to make a telepathy call?'

'I believe I am, yes,' responded LJM.

'And these three women are the recipients of your calls.'

'Yes, I refer to them jokingly sometimes as my harem,' said LJM honestly.

'Why only women?'

'I don't know. It just turns out that way. Anisa was a fourth recipient. If you ask Patsy, she'll tell you that she's managed to get in contact with a man called Derek.'

'What about negative mass?'

'We're all confirmed carriers of negative mass,' confirmed LJM.

The details of the liver had been deliberately withheld from the press release, so LJM didn't enlighten them. That would be their little secret.

'How much negative mass?' 'That's private,' stated LJM.

'Thank you. That will be all for now.'

When the time came to make the trip to the UK, it was decided that they would send the carriers on two separate jets. This was to minimise the weather risk. This was the other aspect that was kept secret. Seeing as the risk was unquantified, there seemed little point in scaring people. Let them swallow negative mass and telepathy first.

So LJM went with Patsy and Shanice went with Geraldine.

The press was waiting again for them when they arrived on the tarmac.

'Any reason for the two jets? Please, we want to understand why you travelled separately.'

'Patsy and I are getting married,' joked LJM. He got a poke in the ribs from Patsy.

'Is that true, Patsy, that you and Bob are getting married?' No answer.

'How about doing a telepathy call for us?'

'That probably won't work,' said LJM. 'Why not?'

'Because you suggested it,' retorted LJM. 'At least go through the motions for us.' 'Oh, all right.' LJM sighed.

He got down on the tarmac and prayed face down, then he prayed face up. To his surprise, he got someone.

'Hi, Dad, it's Alex. I heard you were coming to the UK. I thought I'd give this telepathy a go. It really works, doesn't it?'

'Hi, Alex, it's Dad. Yes, it looks like you've successfully initiated a call with me. I don't know how you got your timing because I've only just got off a plane.'

'I just sort of played it by intuition. This is wicked.' 'Yes, it's great fun. Everything else OK?'

'Yes, I'm fine. Hope you are too. Lots of love, Alex.' 'Bye and lots of love, Dad.'

'Who was that?' asked the press. 'My son,' said LJM truthfully.

'So your children are carriers too?'

Silence. They weren't supposed to know that.

It occurred to LJM that he couldn't really tell who had initiated the call. Perhaps that was one distinction too far from the physics crowd, and maybe it didn't really work that way. Maybe it was just a simultaneous occurrence of two people trying to get in contact without necessarily knowing who was on the other end. Either way, there was no bill to pay!

LJM and Patsy then got into the secret service car that was waiting by the plane. No need for customs. Everything was authorised in advance. The same drill was used for Shanice and Geraldine when their plane arrived.

They drove to Exeter separately. It was impractical to have two simultaneous jets for such a small airport, so this was the best way of maintaining separation and minimising weather risk.

LJM was well used to the routine at Wonford House. He introduced Patsy to the way of things in the QE land of artificial telepathy.

Henning was waiting inside. 'It's a privilege to have two receivers on the project at once,' he said.

'You really want to upgrade us to senders as well, don't you, Henning?' quipped LJM.

'Senders? Receivers?' quibbled Patsy.

'In telepathy terms, you're a receiver if you can receive a message sent by someone else, assumed to be as a voice in your head. You're a sender if you can send a message,' said LJM.

'We must be both senders and receivers when we talk to each other across the world,' pointed out Patsy.

'True. But it's a different story when we try to talk to Henning via his QE machine,' explained LJM. 'We can hear Henning, but Henning can't hear us.'

'I haven't tried it yet, so we don't know about us,' said Patsy. 'Fifty pence says I'm right,' bet LJM.

'I don't gamble,' said Patsy. 'Just know that I'm always right.'

The time came to do the experiment for real, and Henning pressed Go.

'What the hell was that?' exclaimed Patsy. 'Did you get anything?'

'I don't think so. Can we try again? And I'll be able to concentrate better.'

Patsy did indeed concentrate and quickly got the hang of it.

'I can hear you, Henning. That's brilliant because you're not a carrier and yet you can partake in the conversation with the help of your machine.'

'That's not the best news. The best news is that I can hear you too, Patsy. You said "Hello, Henning!"'

'Woohoo!' cheered LJM, feeling slightly left out.

'See? I said I was right,' jibed Patsy, feeling altogether superior.

Henning knew that he would go public with a paper on this. The news that telepathy was for everyone, albeit with mechanical assistance, was huge.

MOODY BLUES

Around this time, LJM had another one of his characteristic downturns where he felt depressed and just wanted to go home. He was informed that this wasn't possible any more, but Black Obsidian would be providing a modest set of homes for them, all on one street. LJM was asked which country he wanted to be home, and he said the UK. That way, he could at least keep up a semblance of a family by visiting his three children. This cheered him up somewhat.

The media rapidly got bored. So what if they could talk telepathically to each other? So what if they measured positive for negative mass? What the hell was negative mass anyway?

There was some consternation as to whether LJM's children should be included in the public list of known carriers. They each had a valid detection but were otherwise invisible to media scrutiny because they carried out their daily lives with impunity. The press did harass them for an answer to the negative-mass question, but they each declined to give one. So they were kept off the radar for the time being.

Whilst they were there in the UK, Derek turned up, having flown in from New York as soon as he was given the news. So Patsy was now a confirmed sender as well as receiver, although Henning could have told them that anyway.

Shanice, Geraldine, and Derek all took the QE test; and Derek turned out to be a sender. This was very important for Henning because he had positive results for both men and women. Shanice and Geraldine were predictably disappointed and joined LJM in mild depression.

Henning explained the results by saying that each person (him included) had a certain strength of sender and receiver. They could only talk to each other if the sender's strength matched the receiver's strength. So a strong sender could send to a weak receiver and so on. Clearly, Patsy and Derek were strong enough senders to be able to match Henning's weak receiver strength, whereas the others weren't.

Next on the list was to arrange a meeting of all known carriers to test the weather hypothesis. LJM's children were all staying in Crediton, near Exeter, for the holidays. So it made sense to go there. The five of them—LJM, Patsy, Shanice, Geraldine, and Derek—got in three separate secret service cars and travelled to Exeter. Henning, Theo, Kingsley, and Julia got in two separate taxis to join them.

They decided to visit Goa Spice to see if the weather event could be repeated. When Harriet, Alex, and Esther had joined them, the Mongols went outside to test the conditions. The weather was stormy, but this time, there was no tornado. And this was with eight carriers in total.

Nevertheless, the Met Office (which was just down the road) declared that the weather conditions were unusual. There was no basis for the stormy weather, and the forecast had been for clear skies. Black Obsidian didn't tell the Met Office that eight carriers were all underneath the storm. So this whopping news remained a secret for the time being.

Black Obsidian did have to rethink its housing plan though. Having all carriers in the same street didn't seem like a good idea any more. They couldn't just explain the original tornado in Exeter as a fluke now with the assessment from the Met Office. This meant that the carriers could return home, just with secret service protection.

When they finished their meal, all twelve of them returned whence they came. For the five carriers—LJM, Patsy, Shanice, Geraldine, and Derek—this meant returning to the Dorchester Hotel in London. The weather came with them.

They'd just about gone inside when the black market finally caught up with them. Eight gunmen in two vans opened fire on the secret service in an all-out gunfight. After a struggle, the secret service were overwhelmed, and the hostiles won. They captured the carriers with black hoods and wrists bound behind them and bundled them out the door into their waiting Enterprise Rent-A-Car van.

Black Obsidian could basically track the progress of the van by the weather effects. This, together with an NM detector sensitive to half a mile, meant that they were able to keep an edge. They tailed the van until Heathrow and then mounted an attack.

In the ensuing struggle, LJM, Patsy, Shanice, and Derek got away; but Geraldine was recaptured.

Several days later, her body was found with her ribcage ripped open and her liver missing.

If LJM was depressed, he was doubly so now. The news of Geraldine's murder hit like a train. They were all scared.

Interestingly this raised interest in the Black Obsidian– sponsored liver transplant operation. Even though Anisa hadn't survived, it was seen as a better way to go than ending up with the hostiles. So Derek put his hand up and volunteered. He travelled to the New York–Presbyterian Hospital to have the operation by the same team as had done so for Anisa.

This meant that LJM was even more determined than ever to keep his children away from this vicious world that he lived in.

Black Obsidian reacted by putting the three remaining carriers in separate hotels. This was to minimise the chances of another all-out attack. However, they underestimated how much they were relying on one another's company, and this only made LJM's depression deeper. In the end, Black Obsidian relented and allowed the carriers to stay in the same hotel. At least the weather had subsided.

The grisly news of Geraldine's murder galvanised the press. All of a sudden, they were on the side of NM carriers in the face of a horrific hostile threat. Black Obsidian did a press release with details of how negative mass is stored in the liver, granting its unusual properties, making it more valuable than moon rock. This explained to the press why the carriers were worth protecting, and they made the headlines once more.

The press were even more on fire to learn that Derek was having a liver transplant, particularly since Anisa had died. Millions wished him well.

In the event, Derek survived, and in post-operation, he tested negative for negative mass. Also as far as he could tell, he'd lost his special powers. He was removed from the list of known carriers and was no longer subject to secret service protection. The success of the operation was released to the press, and they shot a video of his removed liver floating to the ceiling. The intention with all this was to take the power away from the black market.

This was a boon to Black Obsidian because they tripled their stock of NM liver, and now they had a positive message for other carriers, with Derek's ongoing survival.

LJM, Patsy, and Shanice weren't interested in Black Obsidian's offer though. They were all happy to keep their powers and take the risk. For LJM in particular, this marked the end of depression and the start of another manic spell. This was the usual state of affairs for a manic-depressive— straight from depression to mania. There was no such thing as normal.

STORMY MARRIAGE

With Henning working with the QE machine in Exeter and Kingsley returning to the UK to start up operations with the EM machine, it made sense for Black Obsidian to relocate the whole team. Exeter was the best venue for the EM machine, as per the Blue Crystal operation. Conversely, there was no benefit to locating the team in Thames House with MI5. All in all, it made more sense to open an office in Exeter again, with Julia reporting directly to Jack at Black Obsidian.

Julia couldn't get the exact same office as before, so she settled for one in the same building, on the third floor, formerly occupied by Mirada PLC. This was the office that LJM used to work in. So it was all a bit déjà vu.

Henning quickly got into a pattern of doing his paperwork in the office and his experimental work at Wonford House, where the QE machine was located.

Kingsley was starting again and decided that a SuperVan was preferable to a rigid frame bolted-down machine with cast conductor. By using a gel conductor, it was portable, if a little comical, because it resembled a snail leaving a trail of slime wherever it operated. He ordered the latest version from the USA, all a bit hush-hush because it was banned from use on US soil. This cut the Royal Engineers out of the loop and placed control firmly back in the hands of Kingsley himself.

Theo took over software development for both the QE and EM machines. This was something he'd been wanting to do for a while but had been hampered from doing so by the pace of events. It had the benefit of taking the latest versions of the software. Kingsley was pleased because it cut the USA out of the loop during live operations.

First up for Kingsley was a visit to the Dorchester Hotel in London, where the NM carriers were staying. His van included an NM detector, and the idea was to redo all the measurements as a baseline. He had some trouble with the secret service, who were convinced he was carrying a bomb, but when he showed them Black Obsidian ID, they shut up.

Kingsley parked the van out the front of the hotel and pressed Go. All members of the public and secret service within range got caught in a dance of electrocution. But luckily, he pressed Stop before there was any risk of anyone being killed. Kingsley realised he was treading on thin ice by being so fast and loose with operational policy, but his impatience got the better of him.

The results were sent back to base for analysis, and Kingsley caught up with what they were the next day when he drove back to Exeter.

'Kingsley, we've got the results from yesterday's operation at the Dorchester. They show a strong geographical signal in the direction of Exeter, which is to be expected, but they also show three weaker signals from the top floor of the hotel. We don't know who is who without requesting secret service information about who was in each room. We also have the NM detector, which showed four kilograms of negative mass within half a mile. That's slightly down on the four and a half kilograms you'd expect from three carriers, but we'd have to analyse the NM body scanner information to see who it is, assuming there hasn't been any change in real terms,' said Theo.

'Great, so this didn't tell us any more than we already know essentially,' said Kingsley.

'Don't be disheartened,' reassured Julia.

'So where's the next bit of news going to come from?' asked Henning.

'I don't know,' replied Julia. 'If we stick to our knitting, then something will be sure to come up.'

'How about we use the NM detector at long range, say, 100 miles. Then do a survey of the UK to find all negative mass. Then we can improve on the accuracy by going to 50 miles and so on. Then we can use the SuperVan to home in and give detailed information. This is the same plan that they had in the USA but never put into practice,' advised Henning.

'It's more practical to do that in the UK because of the smaller land area,' said Theo.

'All we found last time was LJM's three children and an unknown carrier in Oxford,' said Julia.

'Then we should start by sending SuperVan to Oxford,' said Kingsley.

LJM meanwhile was starting to enjoy himself. He'd shaken off the blues and was getting back to what he enjoyed the most, which was getting in touch with other carriers. He decided he was going to go through a spree of contacting them and asking for name and address so he could follow up later. Either that or follow Patsy's example and get them to travel here.

There was no question of his effectiveness. He contacted the following people:

- Linda in Chicago
- Brenda in Copenhagen
- Denise in Boulogne
- Wendy in Melbourne
- Erica in Manila All women.

Patsy was furious. 'How come you just can't contact men? Look, it's easy. See? I can do it.'

'I wish I knew.' LJM sighed.

It didn't take long for Patsy to forgive him though. She would rather have him using his skills than moping around. In fact, he seemed altogether more attractive than before when he'd turned up in Alice Springs with Sue and then Anisa.

'How about you ask me out on a date?' she suggested. 'I thought you hated me,' came the reply.

'I can't have you trotting off with all those other women,' she enlarged.

'Jealousy, eh? That's a good motive,' he hinted. 'Are you the controlling type to go with it?'

'You know I am,' she admitted.

'Well, as long as we're up front about it. How about I ask you out for dinner. Would you care to go for the Dorchester Hotel?' he responded.

'That would be lovely.'

Kingsley took Theo with him for the trip to Oxford. Theo took his laptop so that they could do results analysis on the fly and home in on the person(s) with multiple measurements if necessary.

He drove across the A303 and then up the A34. The destination was central Oxford so they could get the best fix.

'I don't know why we didn't do this last time,' said Theo. 'Events took over,' said Kingsley.

'But carriers are so valuable you'd think we'd expend every effort in tracking them all down,' continued Theo.

'We didn't know they were so valuable back then,' pointed out Kingsley. 'And besides, LJM has been remarkably effective in tracking down the others. It's cheaper for us to let him carry on and then reap the rewards of his labours.'

'Rumour has it that he's contacted another five women,' said Theo.

'I heard that too,' said Kingsley. 'Good going that man.'

'Now we just need Patsy and Shanice to contact another five men each,' added Theo.

'Rumour has it that Patsy is bisexual and can contact women as well as men,' mused Kingsley.

'I'm sure she's not really bisexual. We're just talking about communicating in telepathy land,' cautioned Theo.

'Who's to say the two things aren't related?' pushed Kingsley. 'In a holistic sense, I guess,' admitted Theo.

When it came to their experiment, Kingsley parked the SuperVan at the end of St Giles, which was a very wide street in Oxford and pretty central. They waited until nobody was close by and then unleashed their load. This time, Kingsley held it for longer because they had a greater area to cover. People in the distance were visibly affected, but not as much as would be close by.

The results showed a strong geographic signal in the direction of Exeter and a weak signal in the direction of the Computer Science Department, further up St Giles.

So Kingsley elected to follow up by parking on Keble Road, just outside the department. They repeated the procedure and identified the target individual as residing on the third floor.

'That's as close as you're going to get,' advised Julia. 'Leave the rest to us. We've got a list of who's in the building, and we can use the latest handheld NM detector to home in.'

So Kingsley and Theo packed it in for the day and drove home.

***

'Hello, Julia, it's Giles.'

'Hello, Giles, what can I do for you?' asked Julia.

'We have reports of the EM machine being used in the UK. First at the Dorchester in London and then twice in Oxford,' said Giles.

'I'm not going to confirm or deny that,' ruled Julia.

'I'll take that as a yes then,' said Giles. 'The prime minister is mightily peeved that this is happening. It would be different if MI5 had visibility of the operations where and why.'

'So you're asking to be notified every time we do something?' she quizzed.

'That's the ticket. The alternative is we make it illegal and throw your asses in jail,' he threatened.

'I see. We'll get back to you,' she finished.

***

Now that they'd cleared some initial stuff out of the way, LJM and Patsy's relationship went from strength to strength.

Patsy copied LJM and went on a spree of contacting new people. She found the following people:

- Brian from Newbury
- Wang from Beijing
- Maurice from Capetown

Beatriz from Sao Paulo Two men and two women.

The Black Obsidian policy was to take their name and address but get them to remain as is to mitigate the weather risk. It also helped to keep them out of the gaze of the black market. Then Black Obsidian sent an NM detector to test them in situ. This way, they would build up a list of known carriers but without the expense of housing them or arranging security.

LJM was so impressed that he proposed to Patsy. He got down on one knee and declared his undying love.

'Will you marry me?'

'Yes,' she answered at once. 'We can invite all the carriers to our wedding.'

'Black Obsidian won't like that,' he countered.

'They won't be able to stop me. I've got all their contact details,' she continued.

'Me too,' agreed LJM. 'OK, let's go for it. Where do you want to get married?'

'At a site of ancient significance. The ancients had more knowledge than we realise, so it's fitting that we honour their memory. I was thinking of Stonehenge,' she announced.

'We'll have to see if our celebrity status can swing that one. It's open to the public every day, and we would have to close it,' he advised.

'Do it for me, darling. I love you. I love you,' she said, manipulating him.

'OK, OK, I'll see what I can do.'

∿∿∾∾⟡⟡∾∾∿∿

Julia announced the result of the search for negative mass in Oxford.

'This is the second time we've tracked someone down ourselves without using the special abilities of a carrier. The first time was LJM himself. This second time, we found Stan from Moscow,' she announced.

There was cheering from the Mongols.

'Woohoo!' said Henning. 'And it's a man too. Do we always find men? Is that our destiny?'

'I don't know about that, but I do know that our activities are being watched. MI5 knew about the Dorchester and Oxford. We'll have to notify them in the future before we do an operation with the EM machine. Whereas the QE machine remains unregulated,' she explained.

'Presumably it's only a matter of time before it gets legislated out of existence.' Kingsley sighed.

'Again I don't know about that. The prime minister, Theresa May, is more tolerant than David Cameron was,' she pointed out.

LJM and Patsy's wedding arrangements were coming along. Stonehenge was confirmed as the location, and the date was the midsummer solstice. A druid would perform the role of minister.

Black Obsidian realised that it couldn't prevent carriers from travelling to the UK if they took it upon themselves, so they simply gave the wedding date and location to the Met Office, along with instructions to watch for anything unusual.

This meant the cat was out of the bag, and the association between NM carriers and the weather was one step closer to being public knowledge.

As the date approached, the number of known carriers increased, and they were all invited. In all, there were thirty of them, plus LJM's children and Stan.

Black Obsidian was expecting something of epic proportions, and they weren't disappointed. The stormy weather dominated the ceremony and picked up at the end to become a category 4 hurricane.

Racism on Hold

The press had a field day with LJM and Patsy's wedding. They had no idea how many NM carriers were there, but they guessed it was quite a lot. And they had the Met Office report for the largest storm ever recorded in the UK.

Conspiracy theories were rampant, ranging from the druids to Stonehenge itself to LJM and Patsy being responsible for controlling the weather. Was the true purpose of Stonehenge finally revealed? Did the ancients discover NM carriers' ability to contact each other via telepathy? Or were LJM and Patsy gods?

Either way, the price on LJM's head escalated. And they weren't just interested in his liver; now they wanted to dice up his entire body.

Black Obsidian asked that he donate his body to medical science in the event of his death. LJM agreed.

Unfortunately, the black market took its second victim when they kidnapped Maurice. This time, his body was never found.

Black Obsidian realised they probably had a leak, but it could have happened when they sent the NM detector to Maurice.

They took a breath and observed that there were far more NM carriers than anyone had suspected. Given that, courtesy of the Mongols, they had a procedure for finding one if they wanted. They would no longer take name and address details from LJM and Patsy, and neither would they send NM detectors to prove their authenticity. Nobody doubted that this telepathy business really worked.

So in this way, the systematic racism that was the hunt for negative-mass carriers came to an end. If LJM and Patsy wanted to contact more of them, then so be it. That was their private business.

LJM, Patsy, Shanice, and Stan warranted ongoing secret service protection. The others were left out in the cold in their own countries. This prompted another round of voluntary liver transplants amongst the newly identified carriers.

Shanice and Stan hit it off and subsequently got married. This meant that LJM and Patsy had another celebrity couple to be friends with.

LJM and Patsy agreed with Black Obsidian that they wouldn't invite NM carriers to the UK en masse for fear of provoking the weather again. They remained in contact, but at a polite distance.

LJM avoided depression by turning to his writing. He added several more chapters to *Black Obsidian* and sent it to Erica Jade at Xlibris for publishing. Patsy was particularly pleased.

Julia held a round-table meeting in the Mongols' office at Kings Wharf in Exeter.

'Black Obsidian have officially shut down the hunt for negative-mass carriers. They allege that this was systematic racism. They realise that identifying them is leading to their death in the hands of the black market. We have more than enough known NM carriers, and we have a procedure for finding more with the EM machine, if we need to. They want us to shut down our operations. Henning, you can continue with the QE machine, but Kingsley, the EM machine is off- limits for the UK at least,' she spoke.

'Well, at least I saw it coming,' said Kingsley. 'I will pack my things and head back to Australia.'

Julia looked disappointed but resigned. 'I'll stay,' said Henning.

'Me too,' said Theo.

Henning organised with Patsy for a follow-up experiment with the QE machine. He wanted to find out the power threshold at which it became effective for telepathy. With Theo's help, he would cut the power in half and then half again until he homed in on the right setting.

Patsy was delighted to be of service, particularly since this was something she could do that LJM couldn't.

After the sequence of tests, starting on full power, Henning deduced that roughly two-thirds power was the threshold.

Given that the intention was to establish two-way telepathy with LJM, if at all possible, Henning reasoned that a machine with double the power should have a fighting chance. Accordingly, he put in a request with Blue Crystal, the original manufacturer. As the inventor of the machine, he still had a working relationship with them.

'How was your day, luscious lips?' asked LJM.

'Lovely, thank you. Henning calibrated his machine, so he knows what is the minimum power needed to contact me,' said Patsy. 'And now he's going to take delivery of a bigger machine so he can have another go at contacting you.'

'How much bigger?'

'I think he settled on twice as big.'

'More random noises and flashes of light then?' he said. 'I guess so,' she answered.

'Well, I've finished with publishing *Black Obsidian*, and now it's on to marketing. I don't much care for it though. I'd rather stay focused on my writing. Accordingly, I have started another book. It's called *Red Jasper*, after the stone used by the Red Indians to make their arrow tips,' he announced.

'So what happens next?' she asked.

'It's more a case of what happened previously. It does a time warp a bit like *Pulp Fiction*.'